"Who gave you authorization to be here?"

She didn't slow down. "You did, sir."

"Me? That's highly unlikely." He again willed his memory to return. He hated this feeling of weakness, not knowing the mission brief or objectives. This woman could be leading him into a trap. He stopped on the stairs and barked an order at her. "What is the name of your superior officer?"

She turned. "His name is Sheriff Tyler Beck of Godspeed, Missouri."

He held on to the peeling handrail for support as her words hit him in the gut. *He* was Tyler Beck, and his hometown was Godspeed, Missouri. But he wasn't a sheriff. He was an officer in the navy SEALs. She was trying to dupe him, capitalizing on his loss of memory to lead him straight into enemy hands.

"Nice try, young lady," he said. "But there's no way I'm a small-town sheriff."

She stood three steps down from him, her eyes running up and down the entire length of his body. "So why are you wearing his _____?"

Elisabeth Rees was raised in the Welsh town of Hay-on-Wye, where her father was the parish vicar. She attended Cardiff University and gained a degree in politics. After meeting her husband, they moved to the wild, rolling hills of Carmarthenshire, and Elisabeth took up writing. She is now a full-time wife, mother and author. Find out more about Elisabeth at elisabethrees.com.

Books by Elisabeth Rees

Love Inspired Suspense

Navy SEAL Defenders

Lethal Exposure
Foul Play
Covert Cargo
Unraveling the Past

Caught in the Crosshairs

Unraveling the Past

Elisabeth Rees

H HARLEQUIN® LOVE INSPIRED® SUSPENSE

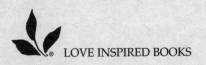 LOVE INSPIRED BOOKS

Recycling programs
for this product may
not exist in your area.

ISBN-13: 978-0-373-67789-4

Unraveling the Past

Copyright © 2016 by Elisabeth Rees

www.Harlequin.com

Printed in U.S.A.

But He said to me, "My grace is sufficient for you, for my power is made perfect in weakness."
−2 Corinthians 12:9

For my longtime friend and ally, Lisa Nicholls,
whose beautiful spirit lights up all the dark places.

ONE

Tyler woke on the floor: cold, hard, damp concrete, strewed with the kind of trash left by vagrants and junkies. Turning his head, he saw empty bottles and cigarette packs lying among half-eaten, moldy snacks and syringes. The smell in the air was almost as unbearable as the excruciating pounding of his head. A bare bulb hung overhead but was not lit, and water had collected inside the glass casing, murky and brown, in which tiny insects had crawled and drowned.

The sound of distant gunfire echoed through the building, and he willed his limbs to move, trying to overcome the pain surging through his body. Danger was close by.

He sat up, speaking his jumbled thoughts out loud. "Where am I?" He put a hand on his pulsating head. "What happened?"

He automatically reached for his weapon, holstered around his waist. He had no memory of the event that had led him here. Where was the rest of his SEAL unit? He figured that he must be on a military mission, but where? His last memories were of dark and dusty hillsides in Afghanistan, of deep and winding caves teeming with enemy forces, of five men fighting alongside him like a band of brothers. This derelict building could be anywhere, but judging by the numerous American brand beer bottles scattered around, he was on home soil. He shook his head, willing the memories to reveal themselves. The temperature was bitterly cold, and he took deep gulps of air to stop his muscles from shivering. It must be winter, wherever he was.

The gunfire increased in intensity, and he hauled himself to his feet with a huge groan to rest an outstretched hand on a nearby wall and steady his shaky legs. Then he staggered out of the room where he had lain and walked a few paces down a long corridor. He looked at the floor. Beside his boot lay a large rock, a sliver of blood snaking down its craggy edge. He gingerly rubbed a finger along a gash on his temple as he realized what had felled him. This rock had not only knocked him out cold, but it had stolen his recollection of events.

"Sheriff Beck! Where are you?" a female voice called out.

He turned his head sharply toward the sound. Beck was *his* surname, but he was Petty Officer

Tyler Beck of SEAL Team Four, based in Little Creek, Virginia. He certainly wasn't a sheriff.

The voice shouted even louder. "Sheriff Beck, we gotta get out of here, now!"

He tried to gauge the location of the woman. Above his head were the metal walkways of another story, and feet were pounding on it, heading in his direction. Inside this huge atrium were small rooms, adjacent to one another along the corridor, and all had rusted bars alongside. It was then that he realized he was in an abandoned prison. But how? And why?

He checked his gun: empty. Ignoring the throbbing of his head, he began to search the ground for a potential weapon, something he could arm himself with. Without a loaded gun, he was defenseless, and worse than that, he had no idea who the enemy was. He was flying blind.

He picked up the same rock that had been used to floor him and lifted it high as he walked confidently toward a doorway that he hoped would lead to a stairwell or an exit. Once he was out in the open air, he was sure that his location would become clear and prompt the memories to flood back. The sound of gunfire bounced and echoed above his head, rattling around the high ceiling. A fierce battle was raging, and he didn't even know whose side he was on.

Then, a woman appeared out of the darkness,

rushing toward him, her face etched with anxiety. She was petite and slight, with large eyes and delicate features. When she saw him, her shoulders visibly relaxed.

"Oh I'm so glad you're okay," she said, reaching out and grasping his arm. Her warm breath sent a white vapor into the air, which suddenly evaporated like mist. "Let's go."

She tried to pull him along the corridor, back in the direction from which he had come, but he shook his arm free and looked her up and down. She was petite and pretty, wearing yellow jeans and baseball sneakers. Her hooded sweatshirt was oversize, and the tiny braids she wore in her dark hair made her appear younger than he suspected she was. The woman was a civilian. Or at least that was his initial assessment.

"Who are you?" he asked, still clutching the rock high in his right hand. "And what are you doing here?"

She stepped back, clearly shocked. "You don't recognize me?"

He shook his head. "I've never seen you before in my life."

She flinched as a shot ricocheted off a steel beam overhead.

She took his arm again. "You're concussed, sir. Just trust me. We're on the same team."

He had to make a split-second decision. Should

he trust her? "You're assisting a Navy SEAL mission here?"

She looked confused for a moment before saluting and speaking rapidly. "That's right, sir. The enemy is closing in. Follow me."

He made a quick judgment call and gave a sharp nod, telling her to lead the way.

"What's your name and rank?" he asked, keeping close to the wall and watching her sneakered feet avoid the abandoned junk on the floor. Old mattresses, chairs and papers lay among spent bullet casings. She moved fast.

"My name is Joanna Graham," she replied. "And I'm a sheriff's deputy."

They reached a foul-smelling stairwell and began to descend. The gunfire was now distant, but still audible, popping like firecrackers in a cavern.

"A sheriff's deputy?" he asked incredulously. What on Earth was a small time law-enforcement officer doing assisting a SEAL mission? He had assumed she was CIA or FBI, but never a sheriff's deputy. "You're seriously out of your depth, Deputy. Who gave you authorization to be here?"

She didn't slow down. "You did, sir."

"Me? That's highly unlikely." He again willed his memory to return. He hated this feeling of weakness, not knowing the mission brief or objectives. This woman could be leading him into a trap. He stopped on the stairs and barked an order at her. "What is the name of your superior officer?"

She turned. "His name is Sheriff Tyler Beck of Godspeed, Missouri."

He held on to the peeling handrail for support as her words hit him in the gut. *He* was Tyler Beck and his hometown was Godspeed, Missouri. But he wasn't a sheriff. He was an officer in the Navy SEALs. She was trying to dupe him, capitalizing on his loss of memory to lead him straight into enemy hands.

"Nice try, young lady," he said. "But there's no way I'm a small-town sheriff."

She stood three steps down from him, her eyes running up and down the length of his body. "So why are you wearing his uniform?"

Deputy Joanna Graham yanked her confused and ashen-faced sheriff outside, taking a huge lungful of the cold evening air. Sheriff Beck was staring down at his clothes as if he couldn't quite believe the story she was telling him. Something had snatched away years of his memories. Tyler had responded to her panicked and desperate call for help after she discovered that she'd been ratted out on her undercover assignment. From a cell window, she had watched his cruiser speed down the old prison road, but she had no idea what happened to him once he got inside. What could have occurred to cause this memory loss? The dark, sticky blood in his sandy hair gave her a good clue.

Joanna had spent many months infiltrating a notorious meth gang, The Scorpions, so called because of the distinctive scorpion logo placed on all their merchandise. She'd worked hard to learn their customs and codes, and earn their trust, only for all her hard work to be wiped away in the blink of an eye when she was confronted with the barrel of a gun. Her first venture into undercover police work had led to her almost being killed. And she still wasn't out of danger. Right after her identity had been challenged by one of the gang's leaders, a rival gang had burst into the makeshift meth lab and started shooting. That had bought her enough time to escape, and the turf war was still raging inside. But somebody would be sure to pursue her.

She started running for Tyler's patrol car, feeling the scrubby grass crunch beneath her sneakers. The air temperature had recently plummeted below zero, and the forecasters had predicted a white Christmas, which was now just four days away. Christmas always used to be her favorite time of year, but the season no longer held any joy for her. Nothing did.

"Where are the keys?" she called as she reached

the car, parked under a bare tree. Her heart was thumping. There was no time to lose. "Check every pocket if you don't remember."

The gunfire inside the old prison was now sporadic, coming in rapid bursts, some machine-gun fire and some single shots.

"Wait," called Tyler, seeming confused. "You told me this was a SEAL mission. Is that correct?"

She was breathless and anxious to leave, but Tyler had the keys, and the look on his face told her that he needed some answers.

"No. I told you what you wanted to hear in order to get you out of there right away. This is an undercover police operation organized by the Southern Missouri Drug Task Force." She glanced back to the abandoned prison, huge and decaying in the wasteland, miles from anywhere and a perfect location for a secret meth lab. "I know you find it hard to believe that you're now a sheriff, but you left the SEALs five years ago. You came back to Godspeed to train as a police officer and help us fight the war on meth." She watched him concentrate hard on her words. "It'll all come back soon enough, but until it does, we need to go."

Tyler's eyes searched the ground, as if he might find the answers among the mud and leaves. Joanna had never seen his face so troubled and uncertain. His strength and confidence were usually his best assets, and the people of Yardley County had elected him as their sheriff with a resounding endorsement two years previously. But now he remembered none of it.

A bullet zinged through the air, popping against a nearby tree. It seemed to spur Tyler into action, and he grabbed Joanna by the arm, yanking her to the ground behind the cruiser.

"Where do I keep my ammo?" he asked.

"The glove box," she said breathlessly. "Ammo is there."

Tyler opened the driver's door, scrambled inside and grabbed the ammo. Joanna felt the frost seep through the seat of her neon yellow jeans. She was wearing clothes that she would usually shun, but in order to pass as an anti-government, pro-drug, potential meth cook she needed to look the part.

Tyler reappeared at her side, loading his weapon. He patted down his pockets, finding the cruiser keys in his jacket.

He handed them to her. "You drive. I'll provide cover from the passenger window as we leave."

He seemed more like his old self, cool and collected, and she thanked God for his presence there. She'd initially placed a 9-1-1 call and was told that the SWAT team would take quite a while to mobilize. That's when she'd called Tyler. If he hadn't responded so quickly, she'd most likely be dead by now.

He jerked up his head to look back at the prison. "We got company," he said, a note of urgency in his voice. "Let's hustle."

Tyler crawled back into the car just as more shots from their pursuer rang out, shattering the back window and bringing their dangerous situation into sharper focus.

The sheriff's strong hand reached down and dragged her up onto the driver's seat. "Drive," he ordered. "And make it fast."

Joanna started the car, checking her rearview mirror to see a bald man walking toward them, gun in hand, his face creased in anger. He was known as Crusher within the gang because of his love of fistfighting. And she would now be on the top of his hit list.

She floored the gas pedal, realizing in one agonizing moment that the back tires were embedded in soft earth, not yet frozen by the cool weather. The wheels spun wildly, sending chunks of mud flicking into the air.

Adrenaline rocketed through her. "No! No! We're not moving."

Tyler took aim out the window and fired a series of shots in quick succession. This sent Crusher retreating to the cover of the prison, and the sheriff began bouncing heavily up and down in the passenger seat.

"This should give you some traction," he yelled. "Try again."

She pressed the gas pedal, yanking the steering wheel sharply left and right. The tires slowly turned and managed to grip onto some hard ground. With a huge surge, they began moving and made it onto the cracked asphalt of the old prison road.

Joanna let out a holler of relief. "We made it!"

Sheriff Beck looked over at her as they raced from the prison. "Nice driving. What did you say your name was?"

She still found it hard to believe he didn't even know her name. They had almost kissed once, and now she was a stranger to him. "Joanna Graham, sir."

He turned and reached into the backseat, picking up his hat. "Is this mine?"

"Yes, sir. You've been the sheriff of Yardley County for two years now."

He ran his finger over the gold badge mounted on the front of the hat. "Well, if everything you say is true, Deputy Graham, I'm going to need a lot of help filling in some serious gaps in my memory."

"Don't worry, sir," she said, taking a turn onto

the freeway, which would lead them straight to the hospital. "I got your back."

He smiled. "I can see why I chose you as my deputy. You're tough."

"I was already the deputy when you took over the sheriff's job," she said. "So technically speaking, I chose you."

Tyler studied his reflection in the mirror in his hospital room. Signs of the last few years were evident on his face: a few more lines and wrinkles where none had been before. His sandy-colored hair was beginning to gray a little, still cut in his usual, closely cropped style. He squeezed his eyes tightly shut, frustration bubbling up inside. Why could he remember nothing of the last seven years? Why was his last memory of the Dark Skies mission he had served in Afghanistan? What had happened since? He glanced down at his left hand. No ring. At least he hadn't gotten married. Although maybe that wouldn't be such a bad thing. He knew that he was approaching forty years of age by now. And yet he still remained a single man.

After a CAT scan on his arrival at the hospital, Tyler had been given strong painkillers while his head wound had been stitched by a nurse, who spoke to him like she knew him well, although he didn't recognize her at all. Since she had left him alone, the silence gave Tyler time to think. The effects of the drug were still at work, making him light-headed and woozy, and he wished that Deputy Graham were in the room with him, giving him answers to some burning questions.

The door opened and a young doctor entered, carrying a medical chart.

"Please sit down, Sheriff," he said, signaling to the bed. "You look a little pale."

Tyler sat, leaning forward, hands clasped together in an automatic position of prayer. He found it comforting that one thing he most certainly hadn't forgotten was his unwavering faith in God. This particular memory must be tucked away nice and deep where no amount of injury could reach.

Tyler looked at the doctor and laughed. "Either I'm getting older or doctors are getting younger. You can't be more than twenty years old."

The doctor smiled. "I'm twenty-five years old, Sheriff Beck. My name is Dr. Wayne Sinclair."

Tyler widened his eyes in shock. "No way! You're Bob Sinclair's boy from Addenbrook Farm? The last time I saw you, you were just out of high school. You look all grown up."

Dr. Sinclair sat on a chair and wheeled it with his feet across the floor. He positioned himself close to Tyler and took a tiny flashlight from his top pocket.

"I left school a good few years ago, sir. I'm a newly qualified doctor now. The hospital's attending physician thought that I should be the one to treat you because you've known me my whole life." He shone the light into Tyler's eyes. "We hoped it might trigger some recent memories. You came to my wedding last year. Do you remember?"

Tyler shook his head. "I'm trying hard, but nothing's coming back."

The doctor leaned away from his patient. "While we couldn't detect any obvious damage on your brain scan, it would seem that your temporal lobe has suffered an impairment that can't be seen. This would account for the loss of memory. I understand that the last thing you remember is being on a Navy SEAL mission in Afghanistan, right?"

"That's right, but I've been told this was almost seven years ago." He gave a groan of frustration. "I just can't get my head around it."

The doctor touched his arm in a calming gesture. "I understand. The brain is a highly complex piece of machinery, and we simply don't know why or where your recent memories have gone. But the good news is that most memory loss of this type is recovered spontaneously. It's just a question of time."

Tyler rubbed his forehead with the tips of his fingers. The painkillers had dulled the throbbing of his temples, but he still felt them pulsating, like hammer blows through cotton balls. "How much time?"

"That's the million-dollar question," the doctor replied. "Let's give it a week or two, and if nothing seems to be coming back, we'll start you on a program of rehabilitation." He stood. "In the meantime, there's somebody who's been waiting anxiously in the corridor to see you."

"Who?"

"Deputy Joanna Graham. I think it's a good idea for you to speak with her. She might be able to help you recall some of the last few years you've been in Godspeed. It's worth a try."

Dr. Sinclair opened the door to reveal Joanna leaning against the wall, hands shoved deep in her pockets, staring solemnly at the floor. Festive gold tinsel hung limply along the wall behind her, looking as sad and tired as she did. When she looked up and saw Tyler sitting in his hospital room, she gave him a broad smile, triggering a sensation of warmth in his chest. He began to wonder if they had ever been romantically linked. Would he know if they were dating?

The doctor stepped out. "I'll leave you two to talk. I'll come back later."

Now was Tyler's perfect opportunity to fill in some of those gaps.

"Come on in, Deputy," he said. "It's nice to see a familiar face."

Joanna wasn't sure how to treat Sheriff Beck. He was still her superior, yet he was somehow vulnerable and brought out a feeling of tenderness in her. It was an instinct she had fought long and hard to suppress, since she was always living on borrowed time, never knowing if she had fifty years left to live or fifty days.

She decided to keep it professional. That's what Tyler would want.

"The SWAT team arrived at the prison just a little too late to catch any of the gang members alive," she said. "They recovered seven bodies, and the lab equipment had been destroyed by gunfire. The police are sifting through it all for evidence."

Tyler approached her. He was tall and wide, and often reminded her of a pro wrestler, despite his boyish face. Since his election in Godspeed, he'd become known as the baby-faced sheriff and was popular with everyone, particularly the ladies, whom Tyler could charm to the moon and back.

"Before we continue this conversation," he said, "there's something I need to ask."

"Shoot."

He shifted on his feet. "It's a little awkward."

She guessed what he was getting at. "You want to know if we're…um…you know."

"Yes," he said quickly. "Are we dating?" He looked uncomfortable. "Or have we dated in the past? It's just that I get this feeling around you…" He broke off and laughed. "I feel stupid having to ask."

"It's okay," she said. "We did go on a few dates about a year back, but it never worked out. It wasn't serious. We never even kissed."

"I see. So we still manage to work together and get along?"

"Sort of," she replied diplomatically. "We have disagreements occasionally, but who doesn't?" In truth she and Sheriff Beck made sparks fly but for all the wrong reasons. "You're a man who prefers to play things by the book, and I play a little too fast and loose for your liking." She bumped her clenched fists lightly together. "We kinda clash sometimes."

At first their differences had been exciting, but after a while it had become obvious that they were fundamentally incompatible and mutually decided to end their fledgling romance. But their attraction to each other had never waned, and oftentimes she felt electricity crackle between them. Sheriff Beck regarded her as a risk taker, too reckless, too willing to put herself in the line of fire. But she didn't care.

After an aggressive form of breast cancer had almost ended her life, she had quit her job as a biochemist in Boston and returned to her hometown of Godspeed to train as a local law-enforcement officer. Her parents couldn't quite believe she was throwing away her Ivy League education to become a sheriff's deputy, but she needed to feel more alive, more exhilarated. She needed to mask the dread she felt inside, knowing that her cancer could return to snatch her away at any moment. So she had jumped at the opportunity to go undercover in one of the most notorious criminal gangs in the Midwest. Tyler hadn't wanted her to take the assignment. He'd said that she wasn't ready, but she relished the chance to put herself at the heart of danger. She wanted to live every day as though it were her last.

Tyler's face creased in thought. "I guess if we dated, you must know a lot about me. Why did I leave the SEALs to come back to Godspeed?" He looked down at his uniform. "Why did I swap black ops for writing traffic tickets?"

"Actually," she said, "you do way more than write traffic tickets. Missouri has one of the worst meth problems in the US, and Godspeed has lost way too many residents to addiction. You came home to make a difference, to give us the benefit of your expertise and training. You're a great sheriff, Tyler, you should know that. The whole of Yardley County is united behind you."

"And when I came to the prison today, you were on an undercover assignment in a meth gang?"

"Yes," she replied. "My background in biochemistry made me an ideal candidate to infiltrate the gang and learn their cook methods and means of distribution. I've been undercover for over six months now, and I was really close to meeting the kingpin of the whole operation." She dropped her voice. "But somebody sold me out. When I arrived at the prison this evening, the gang members knew exactly who I was—my name, my rank, everything."

Tyler listened closely. "Were you wired?"

"No. Until you truly earn their trust, the gang leaders check everybody for wires, cell phones and weapons. I agreed to go undercover, knowing that backup wouldn't be an option if ever I got into trouble."

"So how did you call for help?"

"Right after one of The Scorpions confronted me, a rival gang busted in and started shooting. It gave me enough time to make a run for it and grab somebody's cell phone from a table as I passed. I called 9-1-1 first, and then I called you. I saw you arrive within ten minutes, but it was another five before I managed to find you."

"Where is that cell phone now?" Tyler's voice was so commanding, she almost forgot about his memory loss. "We should be trawling through its contacts."

She held it up. "I have it right here. I switched it off just in case the gang can track it. I was going to discuss the matter with Chief Crenshaw when he arrived at the hospital. A nurse told me that he called to check if I was here. The SWAT team told him I'd vanished, so he tracked me down. He's on his way over."

Not a flinch of recognition passed over Tyler's face when she mentioned Chief Crenshaw, despite him and the chief being well acquainted.

"George Crenshaw is Godspeed's chief of police," she continued. "He's heavily involved in the Southern Missouri Drug Task Force, so I figured he'd know what to do with the cell phone."

Tyler's impassive eyes betrayed his lack of understanding. "You mentioned that back at the old prison. What is the Southern Missouri Drug Task Force?"

Joanna shook her head, admonishing herself. "I'm sorry. I've been really selfish. I shouldn't be discussing this case with you when you should be concentrating on your own health."

"Hey," he said in his usual unhurried way. "No apology necessary. If I want to jog my memory, I need somebody reminding me what's happening."

The sudden sound of raised voices in the hallway caught Joanna's attention. She recognized them as those of Chief George Crenshaw and the mayor of Godspeed, Harley Landon. And they were calling her name.

When the door to the room swung open, she knew instantly that something was wrong. Both men looked at her with angry eyes.

"Deputy Joanna Graham," Chief Crenshaw said, pulling cuffs from his pocket. "I am placing you under arrest."

Tyler automatically positioned himself between the two men and Joanna. "What's the charge?"

"Police corruption and drug trafficking," the bearded man said. "And that's just for starters."

Judging by his uniform, Tyler knew that this man must be Godspeed's chief of police.

"Evidence recovered from the meth lab, located in the old Southern Missouri State Prison, shows that Deputy Graham is on the gang's payroll," the chief said. He stared directly at Joanna. "You sold out didn't you, Deputy?"

Joanna pushed her palms forward as if trying to physically shun the accusation. "No!" she protested. "That's not true. If I'd sold out, why would I leave evidence behind?"

"I'm guessing you got sloppy," he replied. "For someone with a Harvard education, you sure can be dumb sometimes."

Tyler saw a flash of resentment in the police chief's eyes, and he didn't like it. This vendetta seemed personal. He knew that he should recognize these men, particularly the ruddy faced, uniformed police chief. But he didn't. And it put him at a disadvantage.

"Back off," Tyler said, becoming defensive. "Let's leave personal insults out of this. What exactly did you find to incriminate Deputy Graham?"

The chief slid his eyes over to Tyler. "The SWAT team recovered handwritten instructions, detailing exactly how many payments this deputy was due to receive in return for safe passage of meth out of Missouri. It gave me enough probable cause to obtain a search warrant for her home." He eyeballed Joanna. "I found approximately two hundred thousand dollars in cash hidden in your closet. Now where do you suppose that came from, Deputy?"

Joanna's face was stricken with horror. "No, no, no," she repeated. "Somebody must have planted that there."

Tyler's mind began to work overtime. Leaving two hundred grand lying around your home didn't seem like the smart thing to do, especially for someone with a Harvard degree.

"Chief," he said. "Have you considered that Deputy Graham might be the victim of a setup? Handwritten notes don't really prove anything. Somebody could've deliberately left them behind before going to her home and leaving the cash."

The police chief softened his expression. "I'm sorry, Tyler. Young Dr. Sinclair told me that you took a blow to the head today and tried to insist that I shouldn't bother you this evening, but I have a job to do. I've been led to understand that you might not remember me." He exchanged glances with the other man in the room, who was a few years older and chubbier than the chief. "I'm Police Chief George Crenshaw, and this is the mayor of Godspeed, Harley Landon."

Tyler knew that these men currently saw him as weak, so he had to change their perception.

"Yes, I know who you are," he lied. "My memory loss was only temporary. I'm fully recovered."

A slow smile spread across the chief's face. "Well, I'm mighty pleased to hear it. You had us worried for a while there." His smile faded. "I wish I didn't have to do this to one of your deputies, but I have no choice. She needs to be remanded into custody until the Feds arrive to take over. I'd rather investigate the case myself, but you know how it is. Small-town chiefs like me get pushed aside when it suits the FBI."

Tyler noticed Joanna rest her forehead in her palm. "This can't be happening," she muttered.

"Why don't you let me run her in?" Tyler said. "I'd like to be the one to do that."

At this point, the mayor intervened. "Thanks for the offer, Sheriff Beck, but that won't be necessary. Chief Crenshaw and I will do all the paperwork."

Tyler narrowed his eyes. "Since when did the mayor of Godspeed assist the police with arrests and paperwork? I know I forgot a few things, but I'm pretty sure that small-town mayors don't have that kind of authority."

The paunchy, middle-aged mayor reddened and cast his eyes downward. "Ah…well…sometimes I just like to go along for the ride." He put his hands in the air. "But you're right, Sheriff. Chief Crenshaw will handle all the paperwork."

Tyler addressed the chief. "Where will Joanna be held?"

"She'll be in the cell at the Godspeed police station for the night." He hooked his thumbs through his belt loops. "It's my station, so I should take her in."

Tyler had to think on his feet. "Come on, George," he said with what he hoped was a note of familiarity. "Joanna's my responsibility. At least let me take her to the cell and hand her over to you officially. Whatever she's done, she's under my jurisdiction."

"Well, that's not strictly true now, is it, Sheriff?" answered George, rubbing his neck. "The undercover operation at the old prison comes under my leadership, not yours."

"But she's *my* deputy," Tyler said. "I'd like to deliver her to the cell myself. Why don't you meet us at Godspeed station? Let's not fight over jurisdiction. Not today."

Chief Crenshaw thought for a moment, smiled, stepped toward Tyler and patted him on the back. "If you're sure you're feeling better, then I guess I can allow you to run her in. Has the hospital cleared you to leave?"

Tyler nodded firmly. "One of the docs gave me a clean bill of health," he said, taking his cuffs and securing them around Joanna's wrists. She flinched under his touch, but she didn't put up a fight. "My cruiser is right outside. I'll have Deputy Graham at the station in no time."

Chief Crenshaw opened the door. "I'll see you there," he said walking purposely down the corridor with the mayor, seemingly anxious to start the process. "Don't dawdle now."

"I won't," Tyler said, pretending to adjust Joanna's cuffs while watching the men enter the elevator. "I'm right behind you."

He then checked the vicinity for Dr. Sinclair, spotting him intently studying brain scan images in a small adjacent room. Creeping along the hallway, Tyler approached the elevator and pressed the button, desperately hoping that the doctor wouldn't see him leave.

His outward demeanor was cool and calm, but inwardly, he was battling some pretty intense emotions. His life had been turned upside down. Whether he liked it or not, he was the sheriff of a county he thought he'd left behind long ago. He'd swapped clandestine missions in far-off lands for local law enforcement in Yardley County, nestled in the boot heel of Missouri. He had been raised in Godspeed by his grandmother after his parents died in a traffic accident when he was just eight years old. His old-fashioned grandmother had taught him to be honest and upstanding and to always trust his gut. He wished she were still alive, able to reassure him that he was doing the right thing, that he wasn't about to make the biggest mistake of his life. But in the absence of both his grandmother and his memory, his gut was the only thing he could trust.

He steered Joanna into the elevator. "Is your memory really back?" she asked. He saw the desperate hope written on her face.

He shook his head. "I lied."

"Even if you don't remember me, Tyler, you know me," she said, facing him with wide eyes, the color of warm dark caramel. "I would never betray you or the sheriff's department."

"I think I believe you."

"But you're taking me in anyway."

He leaned in close. "I'm taking you someplace where we can figure this out together." He reached around and took the cell phone that she still held in one hand behind her back. "And I'm hoping that this will give us some clues about who's behind the setup."

Her face broke into a huge, grateful smile. "You really mean it? You'll help me?"

"We'll help each other," he replied. "With my memory shot to pieces, it looks like I need you as much as you need me."

He silently prayed that Joanna was as trustworthy as he thought, because if she was lying to him, he was in a whole heap of trouble. If he was caught helping her evade arrest, there was more than a good chance that both he and his deputy would be spending Christmas Day behind bars.

TWO

Joanna walked toward the exit of Godspeed General Hospital, past the huge twinkling tree in the foyer and out into the frigid evening air. The festive lights of Godspeed lay before them, reminding her that everyone else in town was preparing for happy days ahead.

"We don't have much time," Tyler said, removing her cuffs and sitting her in the back of the cruiser. "In about twenty minutes, the chief will start to get suspicious that we haven't arrived at the station. Can you direct me to my house? I'm hoping that I keep spare weapons there." He scratched his head. "It's really hard to keep second-guessing myself. This is kinda crazy."

"Head for the courthouse," she said. "Your house isn't far from there."

Tyler slid into the driver's seat, took off his hat and slung it on the seat next to him. He then pulled onto the road, all the while rubbing a hand over his forehead. He looked tense and uneasy, and Joanna's conscience was pricked.

"Listen, Tyler," she said, leaning forward. "You don't have to do this for me. You could lose your job. Or worse. You're committing a felony by helping me to escape."

"I'm well aware of the implications of what I'm doing," Tyler said. "But I don't think you'd be safe in police custody, especially as we don't know who set you up. You're fortunate that the rival gang chose today to launch an attack, because otherwise I don't think you'd be sitting here now."

Joanna shivered, remembering staring down the barrel of a gun. "I guess I was blessed today." She closed her eyes and tried to give silent thanks to God, but the words refused to come, so she gave up.

"I think The Scorpions intended to kill you and then leave a false trail of evidence to implicate you in their criminal activities," Tyler said. "A corrupt deputy would really undermine the undercover operation. But now that you're still alive, the gang will be looking for you in police custody."

The car wound through the streets of Godspeed, and she noticed the look on Tyler's face change as he passed the familiar sights: the library, the veterans' memorial, the grocery stores, the high school, all lit by the soft glow of Christmas lights. A heavy sense of history always lay thickly in the air in Godspeed. The town had hardly changed since she was a girl, and she guessed that Tyler was seeing it as if for the first time in years.

"This must be weird for you, huh?" she said.

He didn't answer for a few moments. He continued to drive, heading for the courthouse, stopping briefly outside the church where she knew the funerals of his parents had taken place over thirty years ago. After Tyler's grandmother died, he left Godspeed to join the military. When he returned, most of the town folks who knew him were shocked. They had assumed there was nothing left for him to come back to. "I feel like I'm in no-man's-land," he said. "I can't move forward and I can't go back." He cruised toward the courthouse. "Everything looks the same, but I don't fit in. I don't belong in Godspeed anymore."

"Yes, you do," she said strongly. "You gotta trust me on this. Yardley County is a much better place since you became our sheriff." She pointed to a side street, dark and quiet. "Turn here. Your house is at the end. The one with the motorcycle in the driveway."

Tyler's eyebrows shot up. "I ride a motorcycle?"

"On your days off, yeah," she said. "I guess you're a lot cooler than you thought."

He rolled to a stop along the curb and checked the street both ways. Then he settled his gaze on her, and she fought to suppress a tug somewhere deep inside. Tyler's crystal-clear eyes, neither gray nor blue but somewhere in between, had taken her breath away the very first time she'd seen them. And they had never lost their ability to draw her in. The sheriff was beyond handsome, with his sandy-brown hair, matching stubble and olive skin. She could scarcely believe it when he had shown an interest in her. She had so wanted him to be her Mr. Right, but it wasn't meant to be, and she had never dropped her guard long enough for him to get close. She infuriated him with her sometimes reckless attitude. Yet Tyler had no true idea why she liked to feel adrenaline course through her veins. He knew of her cancer history, but she had never divulged its profound effect on her. She didn't want his pity. She didn't want anyone's pity. She just wanted to feel normal.

"Come inside with me," he said, searching through his keys to find the one that would fit the lock.

"Take the car around back," she said. "You keep a key underneath a stone in the backyard. I know where it is."

"You seem to know a lot about me, Joanna. An awful lot."

"I guess that's a good thing right now."

"I guess so. Stay alert and let's keep quiet. We'll take some essentials and hit the road."

"Where will we go?"

"I haven't figured out that part yet," he said, starting up the car again and navigating around his motorcycle in the driveway, heading to the back of the house. "I can only take this one step at a time."

Tyler was disappointed at the décor in his home. The living room was filled with hand painted, vintage-style wooden furniture, the kind he'd grown up with in his grandmother's house, and the chairs around the fireplace were high backed and upholstered in floral fabric. It was a home that oozed simple Southern charm, yet the style seemed so unlike anything he would choose.

Joanna must have noted the look of surprise on his face. "Laura from the furniture store picked out most of these pieces for you," she said. "You told her you wanted a home just like the one you grew up in."

"I did?" he said, looking around, noticing familiar items from his past dotted here and there. One item in particular caught his eye: a photograph of six smiling men, his buddies on the last mission he recalled—Dark Skies. That was where he belonged. He was a SEAL. This home was all wrong for him. There was even a Christmas tree in the corner of the room, decorated with silver stars. He never normally bothered with festive decorations. He gave thanks for the gift of God's son each year, but the adornments of the season had never held sway over him.

"What do you want me to do?" Joanna asked, snapping him out of his daze. "We have to be quick."

He headed for the stairs. "I'm going to change out of this uniform. Do you know if I have a gun cabinet?"

"Yes. You keep the key on a chain in the closet."

"Good. Get the key, find a bag and take everything in that cabinet. Then pack some food. We might need it."

He took the stairs two at a time and walked in through the first door he saw. It was the bathroom.

"How can I not remember my own house?" he muttered, taking the next doorway along, leading into a bedroom that he knew must be his. A large picture hung above the bed showing the insignia of the SEALs: an eagle holding a navy anchor, a trident and a flintlock-style pistol. Underneath the insignia were the words The Only Easy Day Was Yesterday, one of the many mottos of the SEALs. Yes, this was his private space.

He found some jeans and a sweatshirt in the closet and discarded his uniform, instantly feeling better for having freed himself of the sheriff's clothes. They didn't seem to fit right. He spied a safe in the corner of the room and stopped dead in his tracks. What code would he use? Bending to one knee, he punched in the ID number of his old SEAL unit and smiled as the door beeped open. Inside the safe was a handgun, a cell phone, his passport and an envelope full of cash. His smile grew even wider. It was just like him to be prepared for anything. He placed the items in a large black bag, along with some spare clothes and stood to consider if he had forgotten anything.

He instantly froze when he caught sight of a shadow though the window. A man was attempting to hide behind a tree in his backyard. Tyler broke into a run, dashing down the stairs to check on Joanna. She was waiting in the living room for him, a zipped bag at her feet.

"I packed the things you asked for, but there's not much food—"

He cut her off. "Somebody's outside in the yard. We gotta go."

"Were we followed?"

"It looks that way." He scanned the room, snatching the motorcycle key from a hook by the front door. He then picked up his bag and slipped his arms through the straps like a back-pack. Joanna fastened her bag in the same way, tightening the straps around her slender frame.

"We'll take the motorcycle," he said. "If this guy's got a car, we should be able to outrun him."

"You want me to drive?" she asked, reaching for the key.

"No."

"You remember how to ride?"

He flashed a grin. "There are some things you never forget."

He recalled seeing two helmets on the enclosed porch and retrieved them, handing the smaller one to Joanna and slipping the other over his head. While steering her to the door, he remembered something vital. He quickly doubled back and picked up a framed photo from the bureau. Smashing the glass on the wood, he quickly flicked the picture of his SEAL buddies out of its frame and slipped it into his pocket. If he had to accept that he was no longer a SEAL, he would carry his past around with him.

The air outside had chilled even further, and Tyler felt his heartbeat pick up pace. The helmet he wore fit snugly, and he could hear the sound of his own blood whooshing around his temples. The remains of his headache still pulsed, and he imagined his brain struggling to repair its damaged temporal lobe. How could a chunk of his life be plunged into darkness, while other memories remained as clear as day? His instinct told him that he could trust this beautiful woman by his side, and his heart told him that he cared about her. But he couldn't be sure. He would need to stay on his guard, just in case he had gotten it badly wrong.

He closed the front door with a soft click and started across the lawn, hoping that the intruder would remain around back until the motorcycle roared to life. A creaking noise caused him to spin quickly. The intruder was at the side of the house, opening the gate that Tyler had bolted behind his cruiser. The pair locked eyes, neither blinking, neither moving for a second or two. He recognized the man's face. The pockmarked skin and deep-set eyes were familiar, and he knew that under the woolen hat was a bald head.

Joanna grabbed the back of his sweatshirt. "It's Crusher," she gasped. "He chased us at the prison."

Tyler pulled his gun from its holster and raised it. Joanna did the same. With two guns trained on him, Crusher's eyes widened, and he raised his own weapon in response.

"Wait," he yelled. "Don't shoot." He lowered his gun. "I'm not here to hurt you. Let's talk."

Tyler rolled his eyes. As if he was going to fall for that.

"Stay right there!" Tyler ordered, as he positioned himself on his motorcycle and waited for Joanna to settle on the pillion.

"If you try to follow us, we'll have no choice but to shoot," he shouted before starting up the engine and drowning out Crusher's reply.

"Keep your gun trained on him," he yelled to Joanna, holstering his own weapon. "And hold on to me tight."

With that, he roared down the street and headed for the open road.

Joanna leaned against the wall of the gas station while Tyler filled up the motorcycle. It was after midnight, and they had crossed the state line into Arkansas, traveling on clear roads like a bullet. But she was frozen to the core. Tyler had given her his padded jacket, yet her teeth still chattered.

Tyler walked over to her, the visor of his helmet threaded through his forearm and resting in the crook of his elbow. He handed her a cup of coffee, purchased from a machine, and she took it gratefully. The warmth of the cardboard cup in her hands was exquisite.

"The cashier says there's a twenty-four-hour motel about two miles down this road. I think we should check in for the night and get some rest before we make a plan."

Joanna glanced anxiously down the dark highway, straight and deserted, stretching into the starry horizon. The gas station was lit up like a beacon in the blackness, with just one lonely male cashier sitting behind bars, reading a sports magazine.

"Do you think somebody followed us?" she asked.

"I doubt it. There's no way anyone could hide away on these roads." He stared into the distance. The sky was free of clouds and as black as oil, lit by millions of stars. "I forgot how special Missouri skies can be."

"I hate to remind you," she said, giving him a gentle nudge. "But we're in Arkansas."

He nudged her back. "Same difference. It's the same sky."

They both stood in silence for a few moments, gazing at the stars, mentally preparing themselves for the task ahead: the job of proving her innocence. She thought of how her life had become a disaster in just a matter of hours. She had woken up that morning as an undercover officer assisting a drug task force. Now she assumed there was a warrant out for her arrest.

She felt Tyler's arm curl around her, and she let her head drop onto his shoulder. If she could, she would fall asleep right there on her feet like a horse.

"However long it takes," he said, "we'll get to the truth."

His words comforted her but also reminded her of her lack of preparedness. She looked down at the bag by her feet. "All I have in my possession are a couple of guns and a lot of ammo." She tried to raise a smile. "And that isn't even mine. I don't have any money at all."

He left his fingers splayed on her shoulder. "Don't worry. I'll take care of expenses. Since I joined the SEALs, I've always kept cash, a passport, a weapon and a cell phone in a locked safe just in case I need them."

"Wow," she said. "I guess you like to be ready for every eventuality."

"The SEALs taught me to always be prepared. Life has a funny way of throwing you a curveball when you least expect it."

"And life just threw you the biggest curveball of all," she said, stealing a glance at his pensive face. "How are you holding up? I know this must be really hard for you, like learning to walk again."

He turned his head and looked down at her. "To tell you the truth, I still can't make much sense of it. I keep closing my eyes and concentrating really hard, but all I see are the hillsides of Afghanistan." He pulled the photograph from his pocket. "I keep seeing these five men." He sighed. "In my mind, this is where I still am. I just wish I knew how and why I ended up back in Godspeed. How could I turn my back on my unit, on my life in Virginia, on everything that I hold sacred?"

"You didn't turn your back on any of those things," she said, positioning her body to face him. "You just took a different path. From what you told me, you thought that God was guiding you back home to Yardley County."

He knit his eyebrows. "I said that?"

"Yes."

Joanna had always found Tyler's strong trust in God uplifting, bolstering her own waning faith. She couldn't see how God would lead her down such a cruel path. She had assumed she had done something wrong and was now being punished. But Tyler's faith was unshakable, and she frequently took solace in it, wrapping herself in his conviction that God listened to all prayers.

He smiled broadly. "Well, if God guided me back home, then it must be for a good reason. I appreciate you telling me that."

He slipped his hand into hers. Tyler was very tactile, and showing affection came easy to him, but she was different.

"You look beat," he said, leading her toward the motorcycle, its blue paint polished to a gleaming shine. "Let's get some sleep and make a plan in the morning."

"Thank you, Tyler," she said. "Even though you're dealing with some pretty intense emotions right now, you're still committed to helping me, and I'm grateful."

He looked skyward, clearly troubled. "The word *intense* doesn't even come close to describing how I'm feeling right now. I'm used to being in control, knowing how to identify the enemy, knowing who I can trust."

"You can trust me," she said. "I promise."

He brought his face down to meet hers. "I'm taking a big chance on you, Deputy, so I hope you don't mind if I ask you some tough questions later on. It's not easy to trust a stranger."

This comment stung. "We're not strangers," she said. "Not by a long shot."

"We're as good as strangers to me," he said. "That's the way I see it right now, at least until my memories start to return. So I'm asking you to be totally open and honest with me, no matter what. Can you do that?"

She imagined Tyler prying into her past, her battle with cancer and the toll it had taken on her. She hated talking about it and usually downplayed her feelings to hide the pain.

"Sure," she replied. "You can ask me anything." She hoped he didn't hear the hesitancy in her voice. He could ask her whatever he wanted, but she might not tell the whole truth.

Tyler woke early, just on the cusp of dawn. He sat bolt upright, taking in his surroundings. He saw a clean, functional room with well-worn furniture and peeling wallpaper, slightly nicotine stained at the top. That was when he remembered he was in a low grade motel, and Joanna was in an adjoining room, connected by an inner door. He checked his watch: 7:15 a.m. He usually didn't sleep so late, but he was glad of the unbroken rest. He rose, straightened out his wrinkled sweatpants and shirt and then rubbed his grumbling stomach. He obviously hadn't eaten in a long while, and he was famished.

A loud knock sounded through the room, and Joanna's voice could be heard on the other side of the door, panicked and insistent.

"Tyler, can I come in? There's something you should see urgently."

He opened the door, and Joanna stood before him, wearing the same clothes she had yesterday: neon yellow jeans, white sneakers and a purple hooded sweatshirt. She would stand out like a sore thumb in any crowd. They would need to buy her some new clothes today.

"What is it?" he asked as she came rushing

into the room, picking up the remote control for the television from the nightstand.

"This," she said, flicking on the TV and turning to a local news station.

On the screen he saw his own face next to Joanna's, above the words *fugitive cops on the run*. He took the remote from her hands and turned up the sound, listening in horror to the newscaster's report: "The sheriff of Yardley County, Missouri, Tyler Beck, is believed to be harboring a wanted felon somewhere in the region, and citizens are being asked to remain vigilant. Deputy Joanna Graham, a former biochemist and Harvard graduate, is wanted by the Federal Bureau of Investigation for alleged drug offenses committed while working undercover for the Southern Missouri Drug Task Force. Both Deputy Graham and Sheriff Beck vanished last night and are now on the run, possibly crossing a state border to evade detection. The Godspeed police chief, George Crenshaw, made this statement about the matter late last night…"

The picture then cut to Chief Crenshaw, standing outside his station, surrounded by reporters shining lights on his face. By his side was the mayor, his lips pinched into a thin smile.

The chief read from a piece of paper in his hand: "'Sheriff Beck suffered a severe blow to the head yesterday while responding to an emergency call, and doctors believe that this injury has seriously affected his memory. The sheriff's actions are entirely out of character, and it's likely that his head injury is to blame. Tyler Beck and I are friends and equals, and I'm not judging him for trying to help his deputy. But I'm appealing to him directly to contact the nearest law-enforcement unit and turn himself in.'" Chief Crenshaw looked straight into the camera, his dark eyes narrowing in seriousness. "Tyler, if you're watching this, please do the right thing. You know it makes sense."

As the clip ended, the anchor shook her coiffured head in disapproval and said, "What is the world coming to when you can't trust your local sheriff's department to uphold the law? These two could possibly be somewhere in the state of Arkansas, so keep a lookout, folks, and if you spot them, do not approach them. Instead call 9-1-1 right away. But don't let this news stop you from enjoying the Christmas holidays. Go out and continue your shopping, but be vigilant. Stay safe."

Tyler let out a long breath, as if he had been winded. He never expected this amount of publicity. He knew that Chief Crenshaw would be annoyed at being duped, but to place Joanna in further danger like this was just plain irresponsible. Crenshaw had now totally exposed her as an undercover officer. If any members of The Scorpions didn't already know her status as a sheriff's deputy, they would now, and they might decide to exact their own vengeance.

"Do you think the guy who checked us into the motel last night will call the police?" Joanna asked.

"It was late, dark and he was only a teenager, more interested in playing his computer game than looking at our faces." Tyler wasn't totally convinced of this, but he hoped it was true. "We should hit the road anyway, just in case."

Joanna raked her hands through her long, dark hair. She had removed the tiny braids she had worn the previous day, and the strands were now slightly crinkled yet still lustrous and shiny, falling like silk over her shoulders. Something stirred in his memory: a flicker of recollection. He knew how her hair smelled and how it felt beneath his touch.

"Where can we go?" she asked. "Our faces are splashed all over the news."

Tyler pulled the photograph from his pocket. The five other men in this picture were as good as family to him, and he would trust each of them with his life. With one of them now dead, this left four people to whom he could reach out for help. He knew each of their cell phone numbers by heart, but he had lost seven years. Would they have moved on without his knowing? Would they still have the bonds of friendship they once did?

He took out his cell phone. "I'm gonna make a call. Don't go anywhere," he said walking into the bathroom, closing the door and sitting on the edge of the tub. He didn't feel entirely comfortable making this call in front of Joanna. He figured he could almost certainly trust her, but there was still a tiny seed of suspicion, a niggling doubt that she was holding back somehow. When he had asked her to be completely honest with him, he had sensed her reticence and suspected that she was holding something back. Despite her apparent openness, there was something aloof about her, a part that she kept hidden. He pondered whether this was the reason for their breakup. One character trait he would not tolerate was an inclination to lie. Joanna had not fully passed his test. Not yet.

He punched in the number of Dillon Randall, a close friend and colleague who had served alongside him on at least three missions that he could remember. A recorded message told him that the number had been disconnected. He tried the other three numbers and got the same result. The data in his head must be old and out of date.

He clicked his tongue in exasperation, feeling the time ticking by. He should take Joanna away from this place and get her somewhere safer, but without a plan, he could simply make things worse by moving her out in the open.

He turned over the photograph in his hands, thinking hard, and caught sight of a scrawled number on the back. His heart lifted. It was his own writing, and above the number was one single word: *Blade*. What did this mean? Whose number was it? Given that his options were limited, he decided to give it a try.

When the phone was answered Tyler recognized his old friend Edward Harding's voice instantly, his laid back, relaxed style of talking making his *hello* sound like the word *yellow.*

"Hi," he said quickly. "It's Tyler."

Ed's tone instantly changed to a sociable one. "Hey, Sheriff. How is everything in Yardley County?"

"Listen, Ed," Tyler began. "I need help."

Ed remained silent for a few seconds before answering. "Everything okay, Tyler? Nobody's called me by the name Ed in a long time."

"What do you mean?" Tyler asked, confused. "Did you change your name?"

"Um, not exactly," Ed replied with a note of concern. "But since I lost my leg, my buddies all call me Blade, remember?"

"What!" Tyler exclaimed. How could he have forgotten something like this? "You lost a leg?"

"Yeah, right after Dark Skies. What's going on, Tyler? What happened to you?"

Tyler stared down at the photograph, now understanding why he had written the word *Blade* above the number. "I somehow lost the last seven years of my life," he said. "And now I'm on the run from the police, trying to protect a deputy who's been wrongly accused of a crime, and my face is all over the local news."

Ed obviously took a little while to let this information sink in. "I'm not even gonna ask how this happened," he said finally. "Because I'm guessing you don't have a lot of time. You need somewhere to hole up, right?"

"Right."

"Where are you?"

"Northern Arkansas."

"Are you close to Millington, Tennessee?"

Tyler pictured a map of the area in his mind. "Yeah, it's only a couple of hours away. There's a naval base there."

"That's right. The navy sometimes uses the base for top-secret training, and they own a log cabin in the Meeman-Shelby Forest State Park for secret personnel to stay away from prying eyes. I went there once before I was medically discharged—"

Tyler cut him off. "You're not a SEAL anymore?"

"Tyler," Ed replied with a low laugh, "I just told you that I only have one leg."

In spite of his situation, Tyler laughed, too. "I'm sorry, Ed, this is a lot to take in."

"I might need to call in a favor or two to gain access to the cabin. I'll contact Dillon. He transferred into the coast guard a little while back, but he's a lieutenant now, and he'll be able to pull a few strings."

Tyler felt a swell of gratitude in his chest. "I realize I'm asking you to take a big risk."

Ed came back quickly with the words of a SEAL motto. "He who is not courageous enough to take risks…"

Tyler finished the sentence: "Will accomplish nothing in life."

"Exactly, my friend. Go to the state park and keep your cell phone on. I'm in North Carolina, so it'll take me nine or ten hours to reach you by car, but I'll get there."

The faint sounds of a police siren drifted into the bathroom. Tyler inhaled sharply. Had the sullen teenager at the reception desk recognized them after all?

"I gotta go," he said. "I hear sirens."

If any gang members listened to police scanners, it could mean that Crusher might not be far behind.

"Go," Ed said firmly. "But remember—*Audentes Fortuna Iuvat*."

Tyler translated the Latin phrase that his SEAL

team would often recite before missions: "Fortune favors the brave."

He ended the call, flung open the bathroom door and picked up his motorcycle key from the dresser, ready to jump into action. Tyler may have lost a significant portion of his life, but he most definitely remembered how to be brave.

THREE

A flutter rose in Joanna's chest as she realized that she and Tyler were trapped. Two police vehicles had screeched to a halt outside the motel, and four armed officers stood by the cars while the skinny teenager from the front desk pointed up to their rooms on the second floor.

"They're here for us," she said, feeling her heart begin to pound, galvanizing her into action. "They're coming up the stairs."

Tyler grabbed her arm and led her into the bathroom. "I already anticipated this, so I parked the motorcycle around back late last night and hid the helmets in the bushes."

Before Joanna knew what was happening, he had lifted her up and was pushing her through the bathroom window onto the fire escape. The metal was covered with a white frost, glinting in the winter sun. The two black bags containing their weapons and Tyler's personal items were pushed through next. They thudded on the

metal landing, closely followed by Tyler himself.
He yanked the overhead fire escape ladder and
pulled hard, sending it sliding to the ground in a
whooshing movement.

"You first," he said, directing her to place her
feet on the ladder while he threw the bags onto
the grass below. "Don't panic but move fast. I'll
be just behind you."

Joanna felt her feet slip on the rungs in her
sneakers. These shoes weren't made to be functional; they were made to look fashionable, and
the grip was useless, particularly on the slippery
metal.

"Stay calm," Tyler urged, seeing her stumble
and hold tight with freezing fingers onto the sides
of the ladder. "I'm right here."

"I'm plenty calm," she muttered, feeling a little
irritated. "I'm doing fine."

Why did her sheriff never seem to see her as
strong and capable? No matter how hard she
tried, he always assumed she would mess up.
He sometimes infuriated her.

Up above their heads, she heard loud knocks
on the door of their motel room, followed by the
words, "Open up. This is the police."

Joanna reached the last rung of the ladder and
dropped to the hardened ground as gracefully as
a cat. Then she pulled her weapon from its holster and began to scan the area, searching for

any hostiles. She found none, yet she felt the familiar tingle of excitement in her belly that only came from confronting danger head-on. It filled her up. It occupied those parts that were empty and hollow.

It was only when Tyler's voice broke through her thoughts that she realized she had been lost in her own world, tensed up, ready to tackle imminent threats.

"Joanna," he called from the motorcycle, holding a helmet in his hand. "Put this on and let's go." He glanced upward and she did the same, seeing the face of a police officer peering out the open bathroom window.

"Stop right there!" the officer yelled. "You're under arrest."

Tyler started up the motorcycle and flicked the kickstand with his foot. Joanna had no time to secure the fastenings of the helmet. She flung the straps of a bag around her shoulders and sprang onto the pillion. Tyler accelerated so fast that she almost lost her balance with the thrusting power of the engine. She was forced to grip his waist tightly as he took the motorcycle over the frost-tipped grass and onto the parking lot. The tires squealed loudly, as Tyler changed direction quickly to take them out onto the highway, heading northeast, back toward the Missouri border. She felt exhilarated, with the wind rushing through her open visor and the sound of the engine rumbling beneath the tires. They had escaped.

She glanced behind to see the officers scrambling to get into their vehicles and pursue, but their patrol cars were no match for the speed of Tyler's powerful motorcycle. Within seconds, the cruisers were little more than dots in the distance, red and blue lights flashing in the early-morning haze. Yet the officers would be calling for backup. More would come. She hoped that Tyler had a plan because heading for the Missouri border probably wasn't in their best interest.

Tyler clearly did have a plan, as no sooner had the thought entered her mind than he switched direction, exiting the highway and taking them onto a back road. They were now on an eastward path, leading to Tennessee. She watched the greenery whizz by in a blur of color, allowing her senses to calm once more. Being in close physical proximity to danger was the only way she could feel part of the human race. It seemed to be the only way she could feel much of anything.

As soon as the opportunity arose, Tyler pulled into a deserted rest area and guided the motorcycle to a secluded spot behind a bathroom block. He cut the engine and she took off her helmet, rubbing her hands together for warmth. Her face was numb.

"Wow, that was exciting," she said. "What a rush."

Tyler slid his helmet from his head, his sandy hair bouncing with the movement. His face was angry. "No, that was *not* a rush," he said forcefully. "It was a really close call, and you need to start paying better attention to your surroundings. You're way too careless."

She rolled her eyes. She had heard this speech many times from Tyler: she was too careless, reckless, irresponsible and a whole bunch of other adjectives that were variations on the same theme.

"What did I do this time?" she asked. "Did I fail to lace up my sneakers with a safe and secure double knot?" She knew she was being childish, but Tyler often hit a nerve.

He pointed down the quiet road. "Crusher was there at the motel."

Joanna flung a hand up to her face. "What? Crusher? Where?"

"He was in a car in the parking lot, just sitting there, watching."

She felt sure she had scanned the area thoroughly. "Are you sure? I took a good look around."

"No, you didn't," Tyler said, raising his voice. "You *think* you were on your guard, but in reality, you were unfocused and sloppy. At one point I actually thought you were enjoying the dangerous situation."

Joanna shrugged. "I wasn't enjoying it," she said, feeling the need to defend herself. "But neither was I scared. I thought bravery was a good attribute to have."

"Being brave is not about being gung ho," Tyler said, speaking quietly and slowly, as if trying to contain his irritation. "It's about being able to defend yourself properly. Crusher was right there in front of us, and you didn't see him because you were caught up in the moment. He could have fired on you or pursued us or tried to run us down."

"But he didn't," she argued.

"And that's probably because there were two police cars sitting only yards away from him." She could see Tyler's frustration bubbling. "We were fortunate this time. Crusher has no idea what direction we took from the highway. You should always remember that bravery is not the same as recklessness."

She smiled.

"Did I say something funny?" Tyler asked, crossing his arms.

"You said those exact same words to me seven months ago," she replied. "Right before I went undercover with The Scorpions. You didn't want me to take the job. You said I wasn't ready for an assignment like that." His lack of belief in her abilities still hurt deeply. "You tried to persuade me to wait until I'd undergone more intensive training before agreeing to any undercover work."

He raised his eyebrows. "I can see why I would say that."

She crossed her arms, mirroring his defensive stance. They were going over old ground, yet for Tyler it was brand-new.

"Your objections to my assignment were vetoed by the Southern Missouri Drug Task Force," she said defiantly. "And I did a good job of being an undercover officer, no matter how little faith you have in me."

He sighed, no doubt guessing he had perhaps come down a little hard on her. "I'm sorry. You put yourself in the line of fire on a very important assignment, and you deserve far more than criticism. Well done, Deputy Graham. I'm proud of you, despite my objections to your style of working."

She tried so hard not to smile, but it was impossible. Praise from Sheriff Beck was hard to earn, and she basked in its warm glow.

"Thank you, Tyler. I appreciate you saying that."

He checked his watch. "We're heading into

Tennessee where a buddy of mine is going to meet us and help us out. If we avoid the interstate and major highways, we should be okay, but please try to stay alert. If you see anything, and I mean *anything*, that concerns you, tap me on the shoulder, okay?"

Joanna placed a hand over her rumbling stomach. She was famished. "Okay."

"I'll stop along the way to get us some food," he said. "But let me do the talking. I don't want you mess..." He stopped. "Just let me do the talking."

She slid her helmet over her head, knowing the exact content of Tyler's unfinished sentence. The scant praise from Sheriff Beck was short-lived. He had placed himself in charge again, and she was back to being the wild card.

The log cabin in the Meeman-Shelby Forest State Park was perfect, set in beautiful dense woodland, far from any neighboring properties. The forest was spectacular, with a mixture of oaks, American beech, hickory and sweet gum. At any other time, Tyler would be incredibly excited to explore their temporary new environment. But this wasn't a vacation. This was a hideaway.

Tyler pushed his motorcycle inside the garage around back. Joanna watched him with steely eyes, sipping from a bottle of water they'd picked up from a large store in the town of Millington, along with some food provisions and ladies' clothes. Joanna had discarded her neon pants and bright purple sweatshirt and chosen some blue jeans and warm sweaters that would allow her to blend in better. The store in Millington had been full of Christmas shoppers with laden carts, perusing the aisles to the sound of festive songs. The children lining up to meet Santa added to the noisy excitement in the air. Tyler and Joanna must have looked like any regular couple, doing last-minute shopping, and, for a little while, he wished it were true. Spending Christmas in the bosom of your own family was a blessing that many failed to appreciate. Since his grandmother had died, the holidays were mainly lonely and painful, at least those he could recollect. Yet with Joanna by his side, the pain eased a little. The pretense of being a happy couple at Christmas was too much to resist.

His forced his thoughts to return to their immediate situation. He had already scouted out the cabin and the surrounding area, leaving him satisfied that this was the safest place they could possibly be. His earlier heated exchange with Joanna had given him a better understanding of why their relationship hadn't worked out. She truly was hotheaded and impetuous, whereas he was meticulous and measured. He smiled to himself, imagining how she must have driven him crazy—how she still drove him crazy. Yet a lingering feeling of affection for her remained, and he knew that she must have gotten under his skin.

Joanna had said very little while shopping, only asking questions after he had taken a call from Ed, informing them that the cabin had been opened up by a naval officer and was ready for them to inhabit. Their Dark Skies buddy, Dillon Randall, had arranged for the property to be at their disposal until it was required by navy personnel, which wouldn't be for a good while yet. Tyler was beyond grateful. He closed his eyes and said a brief thank you to God for providing them with avenues of help at every turn.

Joanna obviously saw his prayer. "Put in a good word for me, will you?" she said with a strangled laugh. "I need it."

He opened his eyes. She had tried to disguise her misery with humor, but he saw through it in an instant. "You're feeling a little lost, huh?"

"You could say that." She suddenly seemed more vulnerable. "I think God forgot about me somehow."

Tyler walked over to her and sat on the porch step, leaning forward with his forearms on wide apart knees. "God never forgets about anybody," he said softly, watching his breath swirl in the coolness of the air. "Did you ever read that poem about footprints in the sand? When you see only one set of footprints, that's when the Lord carries you."

A sound rushed from her mouth, like a sob, but she quickly turned it into a snort. "Carries me?" she said with incredulity. "Wow, if this is how it feels to be carried, then I'd hate to know how it feels to be put down again."

He couldn't help or counsel Joanna unless he knew more about her, and they had another few hours to wait for Ed to arrive, so he wanted to use it wisely.

"Tell me about yourself," he said. "I'd like to know you."

She smiled. "You know me already. You just forgot all of it."

"Exactly," he said. "So tell me again."

She sat on the step next to him. The late-afternoon sun was pleasantly warming, and it lit up Joanna's face with an orange glow. She really was beautiful, with smooth, clear skin and an expressive face, framed by a mass of deep brown hair. Yet he couldn't see any joy in her heart.

She took a deep breath and stared into the woods beyond. "I grew up on a farm about ten miles from Godspeed. My dad worked the farm while my mom homeschooled me and my brother."

"So you never went to a public school?" he

asked. If Godspeed was also her hometown, this would explain why he didn't remember her from his childhood days. "You didn't go to regular classes with other kids?"

"My mom was an amazing teacher," she said with a note of intense pride. "I had plenty of friends in the area, and I never needed to go to a public school. Whatever I wanted to learn, Mom would show me, and I had a natural ability for understanding biochemistry. I loved studying the way living organisms work, the chemical processes that allow them to function the way they do. The complexity of life in all its forms is fascinating." She clearly noticed the smile light up on Tyler's face. "Yeah, sorry, I can be a bit of a nerd sometimes."

"Never apologize for being intelligent," he said. "Your intellect took you all the way to Harvard. That's pretty incredible."

"I never really thought I had the brains to go to Harvard." She threw her hands into the air. "I mean…me…at an Ivy League university. I was just a hick girl from Missouri who liked looking at cells under a microscope. But I was offered a full scholarship to study molecular and cellular biology."

"So," Tyler said, rubbing his chin. "How does a girl studying molecular and cellular biology end up serving as a sheriff's deputy for Yardley County? It's quite a career change."

"Well," she began, "after I graduated, I went to work for the Department of Immunology and Infectious Diseases in the Harvard School of Public Health. And for the next eight years, I worked on all kinds of amazing projects, trying to find ways to combat the spread of things like malaria, HIV, tuberculosis." She dropped her voice. "And cancer."

"What happened?" he asked. "Why did you leave?"

"I was diagnosed with breast cancer shortly after my thirtieth birthday. It was a particularly aggressive type, and I was only given a twenty percent chance of recovery. I was off work for months and months, just focusing on beating the disease and getting well again. My mom came to Boston to take care of me." She wound her fingers tightly together. "I've never really discussed this in detail with you. I was worried you might see it as a weakness."

"Really? Is that how you see me?" He was disappointed in himself. "I'm sorry. I wish I'd offered you a better shoulder to cry on."

"It's not all your fault," she said with a wave of her hand. "I'm not an easy nut to crack."

"Well, now that I have no recollection of our history, why don't we start over?" He sensed her beginning to relax. "How did your cancer diagnosis make you feel?"

She looked into the distance, seemingly reluctant to answer.

"Please," he coaxed. "I'd like to know."

"Okay," she said. "My diagnosis made me look at my life from a totally new perspective. It's so difficult to face your own mortality, to question whether you've made the most of all the exciting opportunities that life has to offer."

He was beginning to see the reason for her impetuousness. "And you didn't think you'd grasped life by the horns?" he asked. "You felt something was missing?"

"Yes," she said. "When the doctors told me I was in remission four years ago, I knew it didn't mean I was cured. I know exactly how cancer works. I've studied it in molecular detail. If cancer returns, it's usually within five years of treatment, so I'm kind of living day to day just hoping and praying that I'll stay in remission. I've had reconstructive surgery, so on the outside I look perfectly normal and healthy, but the cancer changed me. When I was well enough to return to work, the thought of going back to the lab and handling petri dishes all day was too depressing. I might not have much time left in this world, and I want to make the most of it." She took a deep lungful of air, as if breathing in the vitality of the natural world around them. "I want to feel alive."

"You could have taken up an extreme sport like rock climbing or bungee jumping." He glanced at her, and she shook her head irritably. Maybe he didn't quite fully understand what she was saying.

"I want to make a difference," she said. "Rock climbing and bungee jumping may be great experiences, but they only benefit me. I want to benefit other people. I want to help those who need it."

He nodded with a better understanding. He knew how it felt to want to make a difference.

"So why did you choose the sheriff's department?" he asked. "There are plenty of organizations where you can do good work and help people."

In truth, he was asking the same question of himself. Why did he choose the sleepy county of Yardley over the SEALs?

"While I was working in Boston, I knew that Missouri had a growing problem with the production and trafficking of methamphetamine, but when I moved back to the area, I learned just how bad it had become. It seemed like the ideal opportunity to try to do some good. I underwent police training and joined the sheriff's department immediately." She gave him a broad smile. "But I chose to live in Godspeed for the same reason as you, Sheriff. I wanted to go home. Sometimes when everything around you has fallen apart, there's only one place you want to be, and that's home."

He wondered whether his reasoning had been the same. "Did I return to Godspeed because I wanted to go home?"

"That's what you said when you ran for the position of sheriff. You'd already served a year as a police officer for the Godspeed Police Department, but you didn't always get along with Chief Crenshaw. You thought he allowed Mayor Landon too much influence over police matters and—"

Tyler put up his hand to interrupt. "I noticed that the mayor was standing right beside the chief on the news this morning. Are they close?"

"Almost joined at the hip," Joanna replied. "I rarely see one without the other. The mayor is really concerned with the meth problem in Godspeed, so he takes a very close interest in trying to halt the growth of The Scorpions. He's also heavily involved in the Southern Missouri Drug Task Force."

"That's the organization that placed you undercover with The Scorpions, right?"

"That's correct. It's a team specially designated to deal with narcotics. It's a multiagency task force that includes numerous police chiefs from Southern Missouri, elected mayors and some of the top officials in local government."

"And me?" he asked.

"For a little while, yes," she replied. "But you were quite critical of how the task force was managed, so Mayor Landon forced you out. The board elects a new leader every three years, and Chief Crenshaw was given the job right before the undercover operation began. You said that somebody with more experience in undercover assignments should be the leader, and you caused a bit of a stir. Landon led a group that voted you off the board, so you played no part in the undercover operation after that."

"But I obviously released you from your duties so you could go undercover." He wondered why he would do this if he had no faith in the assignment or those running it.

"You said it was my choice, and you would never try to stand in my way. My background in chemistry made me the ideal person for the job, and I was able to infiltrate the gang by posing as a radical chemistry student who didn't believe in government control. It was terrifying at first, but the adrenaline rush was incredible, knowing that I was putting myself right at the heart of a dangerous meth gang."

There it was again: the reckless edge she couldn't control.

"So what was your job in the gang?" he asked. "Surely you weren't cooking meth yourself?"

"No. I was only observing and cleaning up. The gang wanted to train me to head up a new lab. After I'd been with them for six months, a meeting had been arranged for me to come face-to-face with the boss. They call him Mr. X, and very few people ever get to meet him." Joanna brought her thumb and forefinger together, barely an inch apart. "I was this close to identifying the main player in a major criminal organization. If somebody hadn't ratted me out, I'd have been able to attend that meeting and arrange his arrest. And meth wouldn't still be flooding through Missouri, destroying lives. The Scorpions are responsible for producing about ninety percent of all meth sold on our state's streets."

"So it would seem that somebody stopped you in your tracks before you could identify this Mr. X. It makes me wonder whether the boss has a mole on the inside, protecting him." Tyler knew that corruption within law enforcement existed, and he also knew that the gang would now be desperately worried that Joanna had escaped custody. While she remained in the free world, she could conduct her own investigation and attempt to prove her innocence. She was a major threat. "That's why Crusher is on your tail," he said. "Mr. X wants you dead before you uncover his identity."

"Thanks, Einstein, but I'd already figured that out for myself," she said sarcastically, before quickly following it up with, "Sorry, Tyler. This is a lot to process, and I shouldn't be taking it out on you."

Neither spoke for a while, and a stillness descended. The sun had dropped below the tree line and without its rays, the air grew too chilled for them to comfortably remain outside. Tyler realized that they had veered off topic, and he regretted it. The focus of their conversation should have remained on her battle with cancer. Was this how he treated her in the past? Had he always glossed over her problems and kept the conversation on police work? Maybe he had been too job-oriented, not allowing Joanna to speak freely and openly about her life outside the sheriff's department.

"For you to come back so strong after beating cancer tells me a lot about your character," he said. "I understand a little more now about why you sometimes appear to behave so rashly. And I get why you feel abandoned by God."

His words seemed to have a negative effect, reminding her of all she had suffered.

"When you say that God is carrying me, I have a hard time believing it," she said through clenched teeth. "I was diagnosed with cancer and suffered months of grueling treatment that made me throw up night and day. But I beat it, only to come under an entirely new threat from a drug gang who wants to put a bullet in my head." He saw the flash of anger in her eyes, and he knew her pain was deep. "So if there is only one set of footprints in the sand, then those prints are mine, and mine alone."

He stood and held out his hand for her to take. When her fingers slipped into his, they were chilled, yet they felt familiar. It somehow felt right for her hand to be in his.

"It's getting cold," he said. "It might even snow. Let's go inside and make some dinner while we wait for Ed to arrive. You need a warm meal and a hot bath."

He pulled her to stand, and they walked up the porch steps together, Joanna seeming to be weary and drained.

"You know, there's one fact that you're overlooking," he said, opening the door. "And it's probably the most important fact for someone who's stared death in the face on more than one occasion."

She turned to him. "And what's that?"

He leaned in close. "You're still alive."

Joanna stood back while Tyler embraced his old military friend. She knew of his strong affection for his old SEAL comrades, but she had never met any buddies from his previous life.

When the men pulled apart, Tyler looked down at Ed's legs. "I thought you said you'd lost a leg."

Ed smiled and bent down to knock on his shin, making a hard clunking sound. "They can rebuild you. It's a carbon fiber leg, but sometimes I wear a blade for running. That's why everybody now calls me Blade."

Tyler laughed. "So the upside of losing a leg is that you acquire a cool new name." He rolled the name on his tongue, clearly trying it out. "How did you lose it?"

"You remember the land mine explosion in Afghanistan on the Dark Skies mission?"

Tyler's face fell. "It's one of the last things I *do* remember. It's how we lost Ian."

Joanna knew the story of a SEAL buddy of Tyler's who had been killed after stepping on a land mine. It had affected him deeply.

"That same explosion injured me, too," Ed said. "I got a piece of shrapnel embedded in my lower leg, and it became infected. The doctors tried hard to treat it, but the infection was spreading, and the only way to save the leg was to amputate just below the knee. It took me a long time to accept the loss, but let's not get into that. I want to hear about your situation."

At this moment, Joanna stepped forward and

coughed awkwardly. She felt as though they had forgotten she was there.

"Oh, I'm sorry, Joanna," Tyler said. "I haven't introduced the two of you." He extended his hand toward Ed. "Edward Harding, meet Deputy Joanna Graham. She's the reason we're here. We need to prove her innocence."

Ed approached and shook Joanna's hand. It was a firm grip, squeezing her fingers rather too tight. He was a little younger than Tyler but rougher around the edges. His beard, longish curly hair and callused hands marked him as a man who probably did some kind of hard physical labor. He had the appearance of a strong and sturdy lumberjack, particularly in his plaid shirt.

"Please call me Blade," he said, before turning to Tyler. "And that goes for you, too. I feel like I've gone back in time with you calling me Ed."

"That's part of the problem," Tyler said. "I *have* gone back in time. Losing the last seven years of my life has been totally crazy."

"I'm sure it has," Blade said, sitting on a chair at the kitchen table. "I can't imagine how disorienting it must be to have your memory erased. I'll be happy to try to fill in some gaps."

Tyler smiled. "I appreciate that. Thanks for coming, Blade. I hope we haven't ruined any Christmas plans."

"Not at all," Blade said with a dismissive wave

of his hand. "I have no wife or kids, so I'm a free man." He laughed, yet the hollowness of it was evident. "But I'm not here to discuss me. I'm here to help Joanna, so let's focus on her and make a plan of action."

Tyler pulled out a chair for Joanna to sit. "Agreed. She should always be our priority."

It made Joanna's breath catch in her throat to hear the sheriff describe her as a priority. She never again thought she would be any man's priority, certainly not Tyler's. He had forgotten how much she and he disagreed in the past, how she had continually pushed his temper to the breaking point with her insistence on being the first one at the scene of a dangerous situation.

On one occasion, a 9-1-1 call reporting gunshots had been made, and Joanna was the closest officer. But she was out on patrol alone. Tyler warned her to wait until backup arrived, but she rushed ahead anyway, finding a man who had shot his wife in a domestic dispute. The guy had been high on crystal meth and on seeing Joanna, aimed at her chest and fired before she could react. Her bulletproof vest did its job, but a couple of ribs were cracked by the force of the blow. Despite being injured, she returned fire, wounded the man and cuffed him before backup arrived. Thankfully his wife lived through her ordeal and recovered.

Joanna thought she'd done a great job, but Tyler warned her not to be so impatient again. He said she could've gotten herself killed. Her reaction was to shrug and say that anybody could die at any moment. She didn't see the big deal. She still didn't. Whatever she did, she didn't seem to be capable of winning Tyler's approval. Yes, she was drawn to him, but an equal force also seemed to be pulling her away. They were like the opposite ends of a magnet. They looked good together, but always repelled apart in the end.

"Hey, Joanna."

Tyler's voice broke through her wandering mind, and she realized that she had been daydreaming while he and Blade had been discussing matters.

"You look miles away, Deputy," Tyler said. "You go anywhere nice?"

She shook her head quickly. "Not really." Even in her head, she was always working, going over old cases and calls, wondering if she had made a difference in somebody's life. "Let's get back to business. What did I miss?"

Blade held up the cell phone that she had taken from the prison as she ran. "This is our best chance of finding information that might help us figure out who's at the top of The Scorpions gang."

"But how will that help me?" she asked.

"Unmasking the leader of the gang is the only way to get information," Blade replied. "Once the authorities arrest Mr. X, everything will start to unravel, and several of his minions will almost certainly cut deals with the prosecutor in exchange for witness statements. The truth will come out, and the plan to frame you will be exposed."

Tyler reached over and took the cell phone from Blade's hands. "We can't run the risk of switching it on here as it may have some sort of homing or tracking feature, allowing the gang to pinpoint our location. We need to be prepared as we might not have much time to download the contents before Crusher shows up."

"The data is likely to be encrypted, right?" said Blade.

"That's where you come in," Tyler replied. "You're an expert communications systems engineer. As far as I remember, there's no code you can't crack."

Blade sighed. "That was a long time ago, Tyler. Technology has moved on, but I'll do what I can."

Joanna felt her impatience rising. "Well, it's all we have at the moment," she said, eyeing the clock as it approached 7:00 p.m. "So let's get on with it as soon as possible. We decide where to go, make sure we're armed and ready and leave first thing in the morning. Are we all agreed?"

Blade looked at Tyler. "Is she always this eager?"

Tyler gave a small smile. "Yes. We'll need to stop her from rushing ahead on things."

Joanna ignored the comments. "So where should we go to switch on the phone?"

Tyler's smile grew wider. "I'm always a big fan of returning to the scene of the crime," he said. "While Blade downloads the data, we can look for clues that the police might have missed."

Joanna liked what she was hearing. She was back in territory that suited her perfectly: danger filled, exhilarating and likely to get her heart pumping.

She stood up in excitement. "We're going back to the old prison."

FOUR

Tyler stood close to the television, staring at the screen. Blade was by his side, and both men were concentrating hard on the words being spoken by Mayor Harley Landon, standing on the steps of Godspeed city hall. Several microphones, bearing the names of different news stations, were thrust under his nose and he read from a piece of paper in his hand, taking care to speak slowly and clearly.

"'On behalf of the law-enforcement teams in Yardley County, I would like to apologize for the actions of our sheriff, Tyler Beck, and his deputy, Joanna Graham. I would also like to reassure the public that we are doing everything possible to capture these two fugitives and bring them back to Godspeed to explain themselves. Deputy Graham is facing police corruption charges, and Sheriff Beck will be charged with aiding and abetting a fugitive.'"

Blade took a swig of coffee and shook his

head. "He has no right to call you fugitives until he hears you out."

"Shh," Tyler said, turning up the sound. "We need to hear this."

"'Chief Crenshaw reported last night that Sheriff Beck has suffered a serious head wound, and we believe that this injury may have affected his judgment,'" the mayor continued. "'If he returns to Godspeed voluntarily, we can assure him of fair treatment.'"

The mayor gestured to Chief Crenshaw, who was standing next to him, thumbs hooked into straining belt loops, his face solemn. "'Our chief of police has organized a wide reaching search, extending across state lines, and we're confident that these two fugitives will soon be captured.'"

Blade clicked his tongue in annoyance. "I wish he'd stop using the word *fugitive*. He's trying to turn people against you."

The mayor held up a picture of Tyler on his motorcycle, thrusting it forward for the news cameras. "'Sheriff Beck and Deputy Graham were last seen in northern Arkansas, close to Buffalo City, but they made their getaway on this powerful motorcycle. We don't know their exact location now, and we ask you all to be on your guard and telephone 9-1-1 if you spot this blue motorcycle. Do not approach them. They are armed and dangerous.'"

Tyler became conscious of Joanna standing behind him. He heard her exhale quietly, no doubt feeling saddened at this description. Yes, they were armed, but they definitely were not dangerous.

At this moment, Chief Crenshaw stepped forward and spoke into the microphones. "I know y'all like Sheriff Beck a lot. None of us expected him to put our townsfolk in jeopardy like this, but we have to accept the reality that our babyfaced sheriff isn't the man we thought he was. Let's all remember that Tyler Beck is a former Navy SEAL, highly trained in all kinds of self-defense, so Mayor Landon is right when he advises you not to approach him. Leave this to the experts."

Once the television screen cut to another story in the news studio, Joanna angrily pressed the off switch. "Harley Landon is an idiot. He doesn't have a clue about anything. He just loves giving sound bites."

"I agree," Tyler said. "It seems that the mayor is trying to turn the town against us, using words like *dangerous* and *fugitives*. But we haven't done anything to suggest that we're a threat to the public."

"Harley knows how popular you are in Yardley County," Joanna said. "When we were electing our new sheriff, the people voted for you in record numbers. You're a decorated combat hero.

Harley's always been jealous of your popularity. He only wishes he had half your charm and charisma."

Tyler noticed Joanna's color redden when saying these words, and she stammered to cover her embarrassment. "I mean…um…he's not such a well-liked person as you. You're really good with local people. Everybody loves you. I know you don't remember that, but it's true."

Tyler felt a hand on his shoulder. It was Blade. "Have you noticed your memories returning? Is anything coming back?"

Tyler shook his head. "No. I'm still stuck in Afghanistan on the Dark Skies mission."

"Dark Skies was a tough assignment," Blade said. "Those memories are bound to be the strongest in your mind. Give it time."

Tyler closed his eyes for a second. "It's funny, but in my dreams last night, I was wearing a sheriff's uniform and walking through the streets of Godspeed."

Blade patted him on the back. "You see what I mean!" he exclaimed. "The last few years are all buried in your head somewhere. They've just been shut off for a while."

Tyler smiled, a sense of unease creeping into his belly. What he didn't reveal was that his dream contained more than the simple act of patrolling the streets of Godspeed. He was walking with Joanna, and she was wildly shooting her weapon by his side. He had tried to restrain her, but she had been uncontrollable. He knew it was just a stupid dream, and he shouldn't read too much into it, but it had left him with a feeling of worry.

Blade must have noticed the apprehension on his face. He led his friend toward the back door.

"I need five minutes alone with Tyler," Blade said to Joanna. "Check that you have everything you need, and we'll leave in ten minutes."

Joanna continued to stare at the blank television screen, lost in thought, no doubt still mulling over Mayor Landon's words. "Sure," she said distractedly. "I'll be ready."

Once they were out on the deck, Tyler sat in a wicker chair. "Why do I get the feeling you're about to ask me if I know what I'm doing?"

Blade laughed. "You know me well." He dropped his voice. "Are you absolutely certain that you can trust this woman? Do you wholeheartedly believe she's telling the truth?"

The fact that he didn't even need to think about his answer was reassuring to Tyler. "Yes. I wasn't sure at first, but I'm pretty good at reading people, and I know she's honest. Even though I don't remember her, I know who she is." He shook his head. "I realize that doesn't make much sense."

"It makes perfect sense," Blade said, sitting

opposite his friend. "So if you trust her, why do you look so worried?"

Tyler didn't want to be disloyal to his deputy, but he didn't want to hide his fears. "She's a maverick," he said. "She acts first and thinks later. I'm not sure I can work with her."

Blade gave his friend a shrewd look. "I know. You told me this over a year ago."

Tyler laughed. "Of course," he said. "I should've guessed I would've spoken to you about her. I forget that you know more about me than I do right now."

"When you became sheriff, you and Joanna started dating," Blade said, making sure to keep his voice low. "And at first you thought you might be falling for her."

Tyler knit his eyebrows. "Really?" He just couldn't imagine loving a woman as tempestuous as Joanna.

"Yes, really," Blade said. "But she drove you crazy in more ways than one. You're the most methodical and meticulous man I know, and you said that she was like a whirlwind, never knowing which way she was going to blow next."

Tyler nodded. "That definitely sounds like Joanna."

"When you guys ended your relationship, you were really cut up about it," Blade said. "But you were sure it was for the best. I remember your exact words. You said that you just couldn't trust her not to get herself killed."

"I said that?" Tyler asked. "That sounds pretty harsh."

"You've always been quite hard on Joanna, but it comes from a place of concern. You worry about her ability to keep herself safe."

"What about her ability to keep others safe?" Tyler questioned. "There's always a chance that she'll do something to place us all in jeopardy. That's why I was looking so worried. What if she can't keep her impulsive streak in check?"

"Tyler," Blade said, leaning forward. "If you see her as a risk, then we can make another plan that doesn't include her. This is your investigation, and it's your call."

Tyler checked his watch. "At the moment, I'm prepared to take the risk, because we need to get going and I'm certainly not leaving her behind. She's better off being somewhere I can see her."

Blade smiled. "You can't be with her, and you can't be without her, huh? It's a deadly situation for any man to be in."

Tyler rose and put his hands on the rail and looked out over the vast expanse of green, a huge lake shimmering in the distance.

"I know why she acts like she does, and I want to be patient with her," Tyler said. "But that doesn't change the need for a cool head in this situation. It's one thing for her to place herself in danger, but I won't let her put both of us in danger, as well. If she messes up, I'll have to reassess everything."

"So you're happy to continue?" Blade asked, glancing through the window, where Joanna had come to stand. She was clearly ready to leave, tapping her watch with her index finger.

"As happy as I'll ever be," Tyler said, starting to go inside. "She'll either get us killed or save our lives. With Joanna, there doesn't seem to be any middle ground."

The road to the old prison was creepier than Joanna remembered, strewed with leaves and twigs. The asphalt had started to crack and disintegrate, making the ride a bumpy one. They had wisely decided to travel in Blade's truck, knowing that the police were now searching for the motorcycle. Joanna accepted that law enforcement would eventually track them down—it was only a matter of time—so they were racing against the clock to find out some information that would expose Mr. X and hopefully clear her name.

When the prison came into view, old feelings of fear tinged with excitement flooded Joanna's belly. She had come to this place almost every day for the last six months, using the alias Riley

Ford. The drug task force had given her a whole new identity, even putting in place false records in case The Scorpions wanted to run a check on her. Each day had been a challenge, inching her way ever closer to Mr. X, wondering whether she would be unmasked before completing this vital task.

The Southern Missouri State Prison had been closed for over thirty years. The cost of running the institution had been deemed too high so it was abandoned, the inmates transferred to a brand-new prison to serve out their sentences. The building had been left to fall into dereliction and disrepair, frequently used by junkies to shoot up away from prying eyes. Graffiti covered the walls, and barely a window was left intact. The imposing, dark brick building stood against the skyline like a ruin of an ancient era, crumbling and mossy, behind fences long since cut open. The turreted guard towers were a stark reminder of the fate that awaited potential escapees. It was an impressive and eerie sight.

Apart from addicts, people rarely ventured anywhere near the place, not even the police, so The Scorpions had assessed the building as highly suitable to house a temporary meth lab. They never kept the same lab for longer than six months, and the gang had already identified its next secret location, but Joanna hadn't gotten the chance to find out where it was. Her assignment had ended abruptly and without success. She had spent six months working undercover for nothing. That was a bitter pill to swallow and made her more determined than ever to uncover some truths about Mr. X.

Blade rolled the truck to a stop around the side of the prison, where it wouldn't be easily seen. Police tape was stretched taut over the main entrance, and a do-not-enter sign placed above the gaping space where the door had once been. A gentle flurry of snow started swirling through the air, dancing over the brickwork like petals on the wind. Joanna usually adored the snow. She loved the quietness and stillness that descended with the flakes, muffling the harsh sounds of everyday life. But today it brought nothing but worry. The last thing they needed was a snowstorm to blow in.

"Why don't you stay here and keep guard while Joanna and I go inside?" Tyler said to Blade, checking that his gun was fully loaded. "It makes sense to scope the place out before we switch on the cell. We might stumble across some leads." He turned to Joanna. "We're about to enter a crime scene, so try not to touch anything unless absolutely necessary."

"Shall I take the lead?" she asked, suppressing the urge to retort that she already knew how to handle a crime scene. "I know my way around this place really well."

Tyler glanced at Blade. She didn't like the look that passed between them. Their unspoken words implied that she had been the topic of their earlier conversation. And she guessed it wasn't good.

"No, I'll go first," Tyler said. "Stay right behind me."

"What's the plan if we come up against any gang members?" Joanna asked. "Or any other sources of danger?"

Tyler turned in the passenger seat to look her straight in the eye. "Follow my lead and don't do anything unless I give the order. Got it?"

Joanna felt that she didn't have a choice but to agree. She was impatient to go inside and see whether any trace of evidence had been left behind, anything that might give them a tiny clue as to the whereabouts of the new meth lab.

She nodded. "Got it."

Once they exited the vehicle, she shadowed Tyler's quick footsteps along the path leading to the entrance. Weeds were pushing through the snowy concrete, and ivy was curling up the bent and broken fences, giving the appearance of nature reclaiming her land. And the bracing wind whistled through the nooks and crannies of the building, creating a spooky backdrop of sound.

Tyler ducked under the police tape and entered the hallway leading into the main part of the prison. He stopped briefly to turn to Joanna.

"Remember," he said. "Stay close and don't leave my sight. And above all else, don't shoot unless I give the order."

Tyler really was ramming home his point.

"What's the matter, Sheriff?" she said with a halfhearted laugh. "Do you think I'm going to get us both killed?"

He said nothing. Instead he switched on his flashlight, held it above his gun and began walking into the darkness. Joanna followed, realizing that she had perhaps stumbled on an uncomfortable truth. Tyler was worried that she would put them in danger, that she would act impetuously without considering the consequences. Well, it would be her job to prove him wrong.

"Let's take a quick detour here," Tyler said, shining his flashlight along a narrow hallway that led to a dank and glistening stairwell.

She knew that he wanted to go back to the place where he had woken after being struck on the head. But she didn't see the point in wasting precious time.

"Isn't it better that we go straight to the meth lab?" she whispered. "It makes sense to go where the clues might be."

But he had already begun walking, clearly expecting her to follow. She let out a breath in frustration and accompanied him to the stairs, taking them two at a time. At the top they found a hallway lined with the rusting bars of numerous cells.

"Look," Tyler said, treading carefully. "There are lots of cigar butts on the floor." He bent to inspect them and pointed to the band wrapped around one. "These are the same brand of cigar that Chief Crenshaw smokes, right? I saw some in his pocket at the hospital."

Joanna crouched to take a closer look. "I think so, but I can't be sure."

Tyler closed his eyes, as if casting his mind back. "I remember seeing a man standing over me before I was hit with the rock. It was a big man like Crenshaw."

"You remembered something!" Joanna exclaimed, her voice echoing off the walls. She spoke softly again. "Why didn't you say anything?"

Tyler shook his head quickly. "It's not much to go on. The memory is fuzzy and I can't recall a face. But if these cigar butts are Crenshaw's, then he might be a regular visitor to the prison, judging by the amount here. He could've even been here when I was attacked."

Joanna scanned the trash on the ground. "Tyler, we got some blood here," she said, pointing to a spot on the wall, where it looked like a spray had splattered onto the dirty concrete. "Is it yours?"

Tyler approached the wall and studied it closely. "I don't think so." He turned and seemed to be gauging a distance between two areas. "I woke up over there," he said, extending his arm to a cell about ten feet away. "And my wound was the result of blunt force. This kind of spray would only result from a quick cut from a sharp blade."

He inspected the ground again, his eyes falling on a piece of glass that had wedged itself between two loose bricks.

"Looks like somebody missed this piece of evidence," he said, bending to pick up a chunk of dirty, jagged glass carefully between his thumb and forefinger. "Judging by the blood encrusted on the edge, I'm guessing that this was used as a weapon."

"Do you think you fought with your attacker?" Joanna asked. "Maybe you cut him before he used the rock to knock you out."

"That sounds probable," Tyler said, wrapping the piece of glass in a handkerchief before placing it in his jacket pocket. "We should try to dust it for prints. Mine are likely to be on it, but my attacker's may be there, too."

A clattering noise overhead caused them both to instantly freeze. Joanna raised her weapon to shoulder height and prepared to rush up the stairs to the floor above, but one look from Tyler forced her to reassess her options. She lowered her gun.

"This place is full of rats," she said after careful consideration. "It could be nothing, but let's go check it out."

"Agreed," he said with a curt nod. "I know you had to rein in your first instinct there. Well done."

She pinched her lips together. His praise felt like condescension. She didn't like the way he was trying to change her, to force her to be more like him. They were different people, with different strengths and skills. Why did he assume that her skills were the lesser of the two? She felt as though she was always trying to fit in with his idea of a good deputy.

"The meth lab was on the next floor up," she said, pointing to a stairwell.

Tyler stood back. "You lead the way."

She gave a wry smile. "Do you trust me to handle this situation?" she said with a note of sarcasm.

"Yes, Deputy, I do," he replied. "I totally trust you."

His words seemed genuine, yet she still didn't believe him.

Tyler's heart rate increased as he followed Joanna up the metal staircase to a large room that he assumed was once a recreational hall for the inmates. Black plastic sheeting had been placed over the broken windows, making it a dark and airless space, made worse by the lingering smell left behind by the chemicals used to cook meth. He put a hand over his nose as a pungent aroma of urine, rotten eggs and cleaning fluids hit his nostrils. How had Joanna worked in this place for six months? It was vile. Yet she had been willing to sacrifice so much for the sake of her job. Whatever character failings she had, she certainly wasn't short on bravery. Her fearless nature was admirable, and he knew he should praise her more. He had made a small start on this pledge by allowing her to take the lead in scouting out this meth lab. He desperately hoped that his faith in her wouldn't be ruined by a rash decision or hasty judgment call.

"I don't see anyone," she hissed, shining her flashlight into the corners. The meth equipment had been removed, but shards of broken glass and bullet casings were on the ground among dried bloodstains and chalk outlines of bodies.

A clattering sound echoed in the room, putting them both on high alert. The pair instantly and instinctively stood back-to-back, turning in circles, trying to seek out the source of the noise.

"That's not rats," Joanna whispered, as a shadowy figure sprinted for the stairs, darting quickly in the darkness. "It's a man."

In a flash, she had set off running after the man shouting, "Stop! Police!"

"Joanna," Tyler called, pulling his phone from his pocket and pressing the speed dial for Blade's cell. "Don't shoot."

Tyler began running after Joanna, watching her feet move quickly and silently down the steps. He could see the man ahead of her, racing away, heading for the exit. He was wearing a hoodie, pulled up over his head, and he moved like a rodent in a maze, darting and changing direction quickly with the turns in the stairwell.

"Blade," Tyler said as soon as the cell was answered, "in a minute or so, a scrawny man will come tearing out of the main entrance door. Be ready and restrain him."

"I'm on it," Blade said.

Tyler caught up with Joanna as she reached the first floor. They now faced a long corridor where the running man could be easily seen, his wiry legs pumping hard on the concrete floor.

Joanna held her gun in the air and fired a shot. "Stop!" she yelled. "Police."

"I said don't shoot," Tyler called out.

She didn't halt her pursuit. "It was just a warning shot."

Tyler picked up his pace and overtook her. He was irritated. It may have just been a warning shot, but now they had advertised their presence to anyone who might be within earshot. It was a foolish decision, and she had proved that his faith in her was misplaced.

The man reached the exit and leaped out into the open air, only to be instantly tackled by Blade, who had hidden himself behind the doorway, ready to pounce. The two men fell to the ground in a ball of flailing arms and legs, creating streaks in the fine dusting of snow. It was clear that Blade was the stronger of the two, and he was able to pin the guy to the ground with minimal effort, facedown with his arms behind his back.

"Aw, come on bro," the man said, twisting his head to eyeball Tyler as he approached. "I was just minding my own business. I didn't do nothing wrong."

"Who are you?" Tyler demanded, pulling back the hood and patting him down for weapons but finding nothing. "And what are doing here?"

"Looking for meth," the man said. "There was a lab here that got busted by the police, and sometimes stuff gets left behind. But I didn't find anything. Come on, let me up. I'm freezing down here."

The snowfall had halted, yet the air temperature remained intensely cold. Tyler pulled the shivering man into a sitting position. He wore gray sweatpants that matched his hoodie, baggy and shapeless on his lithe figure. And his beanie hat was pulled down low, right to his eyebrows, where a couple of ring piercings looked red and sore. He was disheveled and dirty, with pock-marked skin, and teeth the color of mud. His story seemed logical so far. This guy checked the boxes of a meth head.

"This is a crime scene," Tyler said, squatting to be on his level. "You shouldn't even be here."

"I didn't touch anything, I promise," the man said, obviously sensing a softening of Tyler's attitude. "I wasn't looking to make trouble."

His eyes slid from Tyler's to Joanna, who had come to stand to the side of him. The man's expression changed to one of recognition. "Hey, Riley!" he exclaimed. "Was that you chasing me outta there?" He shifted uncomfortably on the ground. "I heard you're an undercover cop. Is that true?"

Tyler turned to look at Joanna quizzically.

"Riley was my alias in The Scorpions," she explained. "This is Tommy. He's a regular meth buyer who I got to know from hanging around local crack houses when I was trying to make contacts." She holstered her weapon and folded her arms, taking a couple of steps toward Tommy. "What do you know about my situation? What did you hear?"

Tommy smiled, revealing that some of his

teeth had rotted all the way to the gum line. "I heard you got ratted out by somebody, and now Mr. X has got a whole bunch of his men looking for you. The Scorpions managed to set you up pretty good, didn't they?" His face looked smug. "I saw you on TV. You're a wanted fugitive." He glanced between the two men who flanked him. "So you guys can't arrest me for trespassing because you're on the run from the cops." He laughed. "It's crazy the way some things turn out, isn't it? The Scorpions want to kill you, and the police want to arrest you. Talk about being stuck between a rock and a hard place."

Tommy struggled to push himself up to stand, and Tyler helped him to his feet.

"If you tell anybody you saw us here, I'll personally come find you," Tyler said, bringing his face close to Tommy's. "And that's both a threat and a promise."

Tommy held up his palms in a submissive gesture. "Hey, man, I don't want any trouble. I'm saying nothing."

Tyler extended his hand. "Let's shake on that."

Tommy smiled awkwardly. "You got my word, sir."

"Now get outta here," Tyler said. "And don't come back. Ever. You understand?"

"Yes, sir."

Tommy stood nervously for a few moments,

obviously not quite believing that he was free to go. Then he turned on his heel and took off running along the old prison road, without turning back.

Blade rested his hands on his waist. "Do you think that was a smart move to let him go?"

"We had no choice," Tyler said. "He's right. We can't arrest him, and he's just a small player. We've got bigger fish to catch."

Joanna watched the figure of Tommy growing smaller in the distance. "His brain is fried from all the meth he uses," she said. "Even if he does talk, no one will listen."

"Well, that may be true," Tyler said, still smarting from her disobeying his direct order not to fire her weapon. "But if anyone on the nearby farms heard your gunshot, we may just get a visit from the police anyway."

Joanna looked at the ground. "I did what I thought was best."

"You acted on impulse, Deputy," Tyler began. "I thought we discussed this—"

Blade cut him off. "Let's not waste time arguing about who's right or wrong. I'm sure Missouri is a really nice state, but I'd much prefer to be back in Tennessee."

Tyler nodded. "You're right." He turned his head to Joanna and said, "Our conversation can wait until later."

As he walked back to the truck, he thought he heard her sarcastically mutter, "I look forward to it."

Blade sat in the driver's seat of his truck, pulled the gang's cell phone from his pocket and pressed the power button. The display of the cell flashed to life. Blade hunched over it and feverishly began tapping on the touch screen keypad. He finally let out a long exhalation of breath and lifted his head.

"We're safe," he said. "There are no tracking features on this cell, and it looks like the provider has canceled the service, so it's not emitting any signals."

Joanna smiled. "Finally something has gone our way. So what do you see?"

Blade continued tapping the keys. "There are no contacts, unfortunately, but there seems to be a lot of data here. It's encrypted, but it doesn't look too complex. I should be able to crack these codes in a few hours."

Tyler was checking his weapon in the passenger seat. He looked to be under strain, and Joanna guessed that she was the cause of his tension. She had failed to follow his exact orders, and their clash of personalities had reared its ugly head again. Yet she thought she had done the right thing. She had assumed that a warning shot would frighten the fleeing man into surrendering.

"Okay," Tyler said, holstering his weapon and putting on his sunglasses. "Let's get out of here." His body suddenly tensed, and he put both hands on the dash. "Who's that?"

Joanna jerked her head aside to look along the prison road. There, in the distance, was a car, racing like a streak of lightning toward them, bouncing heavily on the cracked surface. Two people were in the front seats, too far away to see in any detail.

"I thought you said there was no tracking feature on the cell," Joanna said. "So how does anyone know we're here?"

"Maybe your gunshot attracted somebody's attention after all," Tyler said, pulling his gun from its holster again and opening the truck door ready to exit the vehicle. "Or maybe Tommy ratted us out."

Joanna slipped out the back door, shielding her eyes from the sun to get a better view of the approaching car. She saw Tommy, his distinctive beanie hat silhouetted in the passenger seat. She narrowed her eyes and strained to see the face of the driver. A bald-headed man came into view, gripping the wheel tightly, his emotionless face set in a mask of stone.

"Oh no," she gasped. "It's Crusher."

FIVE

Tyler walked a few paces in front of the truck and planted his feet on the ground, aiming his weapon at the approaching car's windshield. Blade stood at his side, mirroring his stance. Tyler berated himself for making the wrong call in allowing Tommy to leave the prison. They had all assumed that this meth user was a small player, yet he had run straight to one of the gang's highest ranking members: Crusher.

The black BMW Crusher was driving stopped abruptly just before entering the rusted prison gates. Neither he nor Tommy made an attempt to exit the vehicle and, instead, they simply sat there, engine running, sinister and unmoving.

Tyler was uneasy. "Blade, you should turn around and make sure we're not ambushed from behind. This could be a trap. If it looks like we might be overrun, get back in the truck and we'll make a getaway."

He glanced at Joanna. "No sudden moves, okay?"

Taking a step forward and raising his gun, he yelled an order. "Turn off the engine and get out of the vehicle!"

The car's engine died away, and the driver's door began to open slowly. A cowboy boot planted itself on the ground.

"Keep your hands where I can see them," Tyler yelled. "I'll shoot you dead if you try anything funny."

A pair of thick fingered hands appeared over the top of the door, hairy arms extending from rolled up shirtsleeves.

"Don't shoot," Crusher called out. "I'm here to talk. That's all. I just want to talk."

Tyler felt every muscle in his body tensing. Something didn't feel right.

Crusher's face was like that of a prizefighter, his nose showing signs of being broken in the past. His heavyset body was strong and lean, probably able to easily lift somebody twice his own bodyweight.

Tyler wasn't taking any chances with this man. "If you want to talk, then talk," he yelled. "I'm all ears."

Crusher looked straight past him and locked eyes with Joanna. "Hello, Riley," he said with a smile. "Or should I call you Joanna now?"

"What do you want?" she called out. "I know you've been sent to kill me, so what do you feel the need to say first?"

Crusher threw back his head and laughed. The sound echoed across the grassland and took Tyler by surprise. He hadn't known what to expect from this hardened gang member, but it wasn't laughter.

"No, I'm not here to kill you," Crusher said, lowering his arms. "I'm here to help you."

Tyler kept his weapon trained on the car. "Keep your hands where I can see them. And get Tommy out of the car, too. I want you both in the open air."

Crusher barked an order to Tommy, and the younger man emerged from the car, hands raised, noticeably shaking.

"Hey," Tommy said nervously. "You should listen to what he has to say. It'll change your perspective on everything."

"I'll be the judge of that," Tyler said before turning his attention back to Crusher. "How exactly are you here to help us?"

Crusher's eyes remained on Joanna. "You and I are on the same side, Joanna."

"I very much doubt it," she called. "I know you too well."

Crusher smiled. "That's where you're wrong. My name is Agent Liam Dennison from the

FBI's Organized Crime Unit. I've been working deep cover with The Scorpions for over twelve months." He jerked his head toward Tommy. "Tommy's been an informant of mine for a long time now, feeding me information that might help me identify the mystery man at the top of this gang, the one they call Mr. X."

"What!" Tyler exclaimed scarcely able to believe this fantastical story. "*You* are an undercover agent?" He took in Crusher's appearance; there was no way this thug could belong to the FBI. "You're a big fistfighter from what I hear."

Crusher's face took on an incredulous expression. "Do you think any man can just walk into a gang like The Scorpions without showing some aggression? They wanted me to go through an initiation ceremony and take part in a drive-by shooting on a rival gang. To avoid that, I had to come up with an alternate plan, so I presented myself as somebody who loves bare-knuckle fighting rather than shooting guns. That way, I could show the aggression they wanted to see without killing anyone." He made a clenched fist with his right hand. "A punch can knock a man out, but it rarely kills him."

Tyler felt conflicted. "What do you think?" he said to Blade and Joanna. "Do you trust him?"

Blade kept his gun raised. "It's a plausible

story. I have a contact in the FBI who could check it out for us."

"My story will check out, I assure you," Crusher said. "If I wanted to kill you, do you think I'd be standing here without a weapon?"

"How come you didn't know that I was working undercover?" Joanna asked. "The FBI should be aware of something like that."

A look of anger passed over the agent's face. "The Southern Missouri Drug Task Force didn't bother to tell the FBI what was going on. They didn't follow protocol or procedure. Before placing any undercover officers in an organization, you're supposed to check with the FBI in case any current agents have infiltrated the ranks already." Crusher lowered his arms and pointed a finger at Tyler. "*You* didn't do that, Sheriff Beck, and as a result Deputy Graham and I were completely unaware of each other's undercover status."

"Don't blame Sheriff Beck," Joanna called. "Godspeed Police Chief Crenshaw took responsibility for leading the assignment. He was the person who should've carried out the proper checks."

Tyler thought of the cigar butts on the ground inside. Had the chief been deliberately sloppy in overseeing this assignment because he wanted it to fail?

"Agent Dennison, has your assignment been

compromised because of this development?" Tyler asked.

The agent knotted his fingers together and pulled them tight around the back of his neck, clearly struggling to keep his emotions together. "Of course it's been compromised," he yelled angrily. "One of the gang leaders told me about Joanna's true identity a half hour before she was due to arrive at the prison, and I was given the job of killing her. I had no time to warn her, so I called a rival gang and gave them the location of our meth lab, knowing they would launch an immediate attack. It was the only way I could think of protecting her. She's fortunate that she was able to escape in the chaos. When I chased you both from the prison, I had to make it look like I wanted to kill you. I purposely let you leave, but I knew Joanna would be living on borrowed time. The Scorpions are very disappointed in me for failing to exterminate her, so they've got another man on the job. He's nicknamed The Dentist, but trust me when I say that you don't want to know why."

Tyler looked over at Joanna. She had wrapped her arms around herself. Did she think that God was retreating even further from her life? These words must be hard for her to hear.

"Not only did Mr. X order Joanna's killing, he made sure to frame her, as well," Agent Dennison continued. "He wanted to totally demoralize the local police and make them wonder how many other officers are on the gang's payroll. Now that Joanna's escaped, Mr. X figures she'll be arrested if the Dentist doesn't manage to kill her first. If that happens, he'll hit her in her jail cell. Apparently, he assumes that murdering somebody in police custody would be easy in a one-horse town like Godspeed."

Tyler finally lowered his gun. Agent Dennison had made a strong case, which he accepted was true. "Wow, this is quite a mess."

The agent vented his frustration. "You're absolutely right, it's a mess." He looked down at his clothes. "Do you think I like dressing like a hoodlum, Sheriff? Do you think I want to shave my head and have bare-knuckle fights with other men? Do you think I want to be freezing my fingers off guarding a meth lab instead of putting up Christmas decorations with my family? I've dedicated the past year of my life to living with this gang day in day out. I've proved myself to them, and they've accepted me as one of their own. But the Southern Missouri Drug Task Force came steamrollering into *my* assignment and rode roughshod over my hard work." He looked skyward. "All of the gang's focus has now gone into killing Joanna just when I was so close to meeting Mr. X."

"I was close, too," called Joanna. "I was due to meet him next week. That's why someone ratted me out. We think there's a corrupt officer protecting the boss of The Scorpions."

"That's a very shrewd assessment, Deputy," the agent said. "And you're almost right. But a corrupt officer isn't protecting the boss. The FBI believes that a corrupt officer *is* the boss."

Tyler felt his eyebrows shoot up. "Seriously?"

"The Organized Crime Unit only puts under-cover agents in the most serious situations," the agent replied. "We knew that The Scorpions were recruiting corrupt police officers all over Missouri, so we figured that somebody at the top had access to police records and was able to target specific officers, ones with money troubles or lifestyles that made them easy to blackmail. The guy at the top of this gang knows too much about cops and police work. He's got to be one of us."

Joanna walked to Tyler's side. "If I'm taken into custody, I won't last twenty-four hours," she said. "I'll end up dead in my cell, and they'll say it was suicide. Whether I'm out in the free world or in a jail cell, The Scorpions will kill me. Nowhere is safe."

Tyler put a hand on her shoulder. "We've got leads to work on, so don't lose hope."

"Wherever you guys are hiding, keep it a well-guarded secret," the agent said. "If you need to contact me, go through Tommy. He looks like a flaky meth head, but he's a smart guy." He glanced over at Tommy. "I know it's hard to believe, but he was once valedictorian of his high school before meth stole his future. Drugs destroy lives."

"And how do we contact Tommy?" Tyler asked, eyeing the scrawny man up and down.

The agent smiled. "Riley—I mean Joanna— knows all his regular haunts." He made a move to get back into his vehicle. "I would advise you to lie low, Joanna."

"The Dentist is the most brutal person I've ever heard of," Tommy said, finding his voice again. "Dennison's right. Stay out of his way. I just heard the sheriff say that you got some leads to work on. Maybe I can help you out if you tell me what you got."

"Thanks for the offer, Tommy," Joanna called. "But we'll do this on our own."

"That's a wise move, Deputy," Dennison said. "Trust no one. The Scorpions have a lot of contacts in a lot of places, and if they find you, I can't protect you."

"She doesn't need you to protect her," Tyler said. "She has me."

"I hope that's enough, Sheriff, I really do."

Tyler lifted his chin. "As long as I'm with her, she'll stay alive." He turned to Joanna. "And that's a promise."

* * *

Joanna flicked between channels on the television, stopping on any local news stations and nervously expecting her picture to appear with an appeal for her to return home. She was thinking of her parents sitting at home in Godspeed, looking at her image on the screen, facing the holidays without her. She imagined their horrified faces on hearing their daughter described as a wanted felon. She couldn't even contact them to explain the situation. It was too risky. But she was missing them with all her heart and longed to feel her mother's arms envelop her and tell her everything would be okay.

Tyler came and sat next to her on the couch. He gently took the remote control from her hand and switched off the TV.

"Don't beat yourself up about the news stories," he said. "You and I know the truth, and that's what matters."

She felt Tyler's warm hands curl around hers. His touch was welcome, yet it also triggered a sense of loneliness deep inside. It was an emotion she had gotten used to. Even when she was in a room full of people, she felt isolated from others. She'd felt that way ever since the day of her diagnosis.

"Blade is dusting the piece of glass from the prison for prints while he runs some code-cracking software on the data from the cell," he said. "He might be able to remotely log us into the FBI database to run a diagnostic on any prints we find. It could give us the breakthrough we need."

Joanna smiled weakly. Usually she was upbeat and raring to go, ready to throw herself into any challenge. But she was deflated, and she didn't want to reveal the reason why.

"That's great," she said.

He squeezed her fingers. "You okay, Joanna?"

"Yeah."

"You sure?"

She removed one of her hands from his and tucked it into her armpit, rubbing at a tender spot. "I have a little twinge of pain. It's probably nothing, but…" She left the unsaid words hanging in the air.

Tyler's eyes flashed with anxiety. "But you're worried that the cancer might be back?"

"Yes."

"Do you want to see a doctor?"

She shook her head vigorously. "No. You heard what Agent Dennison said. We have to keep out of sight." She turned her head to look out the window. "Besides, if the cancer is back, it's likely to be terminal. Treatment could buy me time but not cure it."

"Hey," Tyler said, shifting his position to sit closer to her. "You said it was only a twinge. Try not to read too much into it. Did you hurt yourself at the prison today?"

She thought hard. "I fell against the wall in the stairwell as I chased Tommy." She rolled her shoulder. "I have a bit of stiffness here."

Tyler smiled. "There you go. It's probably just inflammation from bruising."

In her mind, she had assumed the cancer had returned. She had already imagined her funeral. "Probably," she said unconvincingly. "I'm being stupid."

He brushed her cheek with his fingertips. She flinched awkwardly. "You're not being stupid," he said. "You have every right to be afraid."

She lifted her head. "I'm not afraid."

He obviously guessed that he had chosen the wrong words. "Okay, you have every right to be cautious. As soon as it's safe, I'll make sure you see a doctor. I'll even come with you if it helps."

She imagined Tyler sitting by her side, holding her hand, waiting for a doctor to deliver the news that could spell the difference between life and death. It was a comforting image. He was strong and dependable, not likely to crumble under any amount of heartache.

"Thanks," she said. "But you don't have to do that."

"I know I don't have to, but I want to. I care about you, Joanna."

She bit on the inside of her lip to prevent an emotional reaction from surfacing. "You can't really care about me," she said. "It must feel like you only just met me."

"True," he said with a nod. "But there's something very familiar about you. My brain is telling me that you and I have a connection, even though I can't recall exactly how." He tilted his head, encouraging her to look into his eyes. "You're a very special person to me, Joanna. I know that much."

She smiled. "It's nice to hear you say that. I've always assumed I was a nuisance to you, like a loose cannon that you're always afraid will go off at any moment."

"Well," he said, "I must admit that I struggle with the way you do things, but I understand your reasons. You want to live every day as if it's your last."

She pushed her fingers into the tender spot in her armpit, feeling for the familiar, unyielding pressure of a lump.

"You just never know when that time will come," she said quietly. "But I'd always hoped it wouldn't be cancer that takes me. I'd rather die in a hail of bullets than hooked up to a morphine drip, barely able to speak."

Tyler seemed to be considering his response carefully. "Far too many members of law enforcement are killed every day," he said finally. "The last thing this country needs is a deputy who actively goes looking for bullets."

"I don't go looking for them," she protested. "But I don't hide from them either. I have a responsibility to take care of those who need protection."

"Every peace officer killed in the line of duty is a hero in my opinion," Tyler said. "It's a tragedy each time it happens. Yes, you have an obligation to protect and to serve, but you also have a duty of care to yourself. You should take every precaution to stay safe."

She gazed at him. "But my life is worth less than others'," she said. "It makes sense for me to take the risks instead of them."

Tyler's jaw dropped. "What? You really believe that your life has less value than other people's?"

She didn't quite understand why he failed to get it. "Of course. Statistically, I'm more likely to die at a younger age than you because I've received a cancer diagnosis during the last seven years. So if you and I are both facing a man with a gun, it makes sense for me to take the bullet, because you have more chance of living a long and healthy life." She shrugged. "You can't argue with the laws of probability."

"Joanna," Tyler said, cupping her chin. "You're not a statistic. You're a person. And you have an amazing value to so many people—to your family, to me, to God."

She pulled her face away. "I base everything on science, and science tells me that God doesn't exist."

Tyler rubbed his temples. "Do you actually believe He doesn't exist or are you just really angry with Him right now?"

She sighed. "I don't know. A little of both I guess. When I was a biochemist in Boston, I studied some of the most awful diseases you could ever imagine." She widened her eyes and brought her face close to Tyler's. "Did you know that there is a parasite called Acanthamoeba Keratitis whose sole job is to burrow into eyeballs and slowly turn a person blind? How can a loving God create things like that?" She buried her face in her hands, realizing that she was revealing way too much about her lack of faith. This was more personal than she wanted to get with Tyler, but she couldn't seem to stop. "I just don't think I'm capable of being a good Christian." She took her hands away from her face and put them back in his. "Sometimes I rage at God, and sometimes I even hate Him. And that makes me feel ashamed. It makes me a bad person."

Tyler held her fingers tightly. "It doesn't make you a bad person," he said gently. "It makes you human. Everybody questions why bad thing happen. God doesn't want us to follow Him like robots. He wants us look at the world in all its cruelty and yet still place our faith in Him. It's not easy to do. But God is definitely strong enough to take the worst tantrum you can throw at Him." He raised an eyebrow. "And for that matter, so am I."

"Faith used to come so naturally to me," she said. "Back when I thought the world was beautiful, and I was still full of hope. But my faith was obviously as thin as paper because it crumbled away to nothing as soon as it was tested."

Tyler smiled broadly, highlighting the small dimples in his cheeks. "Untested faith is no faith at all. You may feel as though you have no reserves of belief left, but that's when you truly lay down strong foundations. You'll get through this dark time and emerge all the stronger for it. Don't give up on God, Joanna." He locked eyes with her. "Don't give up on *me*."

"I'm not about to give up on anybody," she said, recovering her composure and straightening her back. "I just want to try to make you understand that it should be me taking the risks. I don't mind being the one in the line of fire. At least if I die saving somebody else, my life will have been worthwhile." She gritted her teeth. "I won't let cancer take me. I won't."

Then, without warning, Tyler leaned forward

and enveloped her in a hug. Her senses were filled with his familiar scent and the soft-bristled stubble on her face. The suddenness of his action took her by surprise, and she had no chance to prepare herself. His affection and warmth brought her tears to the surface and, try as she might, they wouldn't stop their path.

"You're a beautiful person, Joanna," he whispered in her ear. "More beautiful than you realize. Your life is full of meaning, and you don't need to prove your worth." He pulled back. "'Be still…'"

She finished the Bible verse that she knew he was quoting. "'And know that I am God.'" She'd heard the line a million times over. "I don't think it's possible for me to be still," she said. "And I don't think it's possible for me to change."

Tyler shifted uncomfortably, as though he wanted to say something that she might not like.

"Whenever you place yourself at the forefront of danger, you're not only putting your own life in jeopardy, but you're risking others, too. Today at the prison when you fired your weapon, that gunshot could have attracted the attention of the police or gang members. It could have been disastrous for all of us."

A sickening sensation curled into her belly. She'd never thought of it like that before. And the criticism was justified. "I'm sorry," she said. "I guess that was foolish. I'll try harder to stay in control of my emotions next time."

He brushed a lock of hair from her face and hooked it behind her ear. "I'm glad you opened up to me, Joanna. It's helped me to understand you a whole lot better." He slid his gaze downward, embarrassed. "I guessed there was something special about you even when I could barely remember my own name. I wish I could unlock all of those conversations we've had in the past. I wish I could remember all the times we've spent together."

She smiled tensely, knowing that he was wearing rose-colored glasses. If Tyler were somehow able to access the memories of their past history, he would be disappointed. Their relationship was mainly characterized by petty squabbles and clashing opinions. She would never have imagined having a heart-to-heart conversation like this one with Sheriff Beck. She was forced to admit that Tyler's memory loss was changing him for the better. He was like a blank canvas, starting over and learning as he went along.

"You know, you're a lot different from how you used to be," she said.

"I am?"

"Yeah, and I like this new Tyler much more than the old one."

His expression was enigmatic. "I'll take that as a compliment." He laughed. "I think."

She stood, rolling away the pain in her shoulder. If the cancer had returned, there was nothing she could do about it, and she would simply have to try to push it to the back of her mind. If she thought that she had a long future ahead of her, she might even consider letting herself fall in love with Tyler. She knew it would be easy. He had the kind of eyes that could melt wax. And he had taken the time to counsel her, despite struggling to cope with serious amnesia.

But she was no match for him. Her body was scarred and broken and, no matter what Tyler said, she knew that her life wasn't worth as much as his. She would try hard not to put others at risk, but she still needed to feel the wind in her hair and a spark of danger in the air.

She couldn't change. She was a lost cause.

Tyler placed a mug of coffee on the kitchen table in front of Blade. The two men had been working late into the night, decrypting the information on the cell, now downloaded to Blade's laptop. Joanna had fallen asleep on the couch under a blanket, and he was glad she was getting some rest. Her concern that her cancer had returned had given him another worry to add to his list. He hadn't been able to stop thinking about her all evening.

The nights in the state park were peaceful, and the only sounds to be heard outside were the calls of nocturnal animals and the creaking of tree branches in the breeze. Flurries of snow fell in bursts, making the landscape appear as though it had been dusted with powdered sugar. They were living on top of their very own Christmas cake, quaint and charming. But appearances could be deceptive, and the beauty of their location could hide a multitude of sinister forces.

"I managed to decode some interesting data at last," Blade said, picking up his mug and taking a gulp. "It looks like Joanna picked up a phone belonging to a high-ranking gang member because there's a lot of sensitive information on there." He turned the screen to Tyler, showing a spreadsheet populated with numerous figures. "These are the exact amounts of meth that the prison lab was tasked with producing each month." He closed the tab and opened a new one: a map of Southern Missouri. "And here we can see the routes that The Scorpions used to smuggle the drug out of Godspeed via a fake courier called Daily Delivery. This company is a front for all the money and shipments of The Scorpions. I found scanned copies of paperwork signed by police officers to falsify the cargo of the vehicles and allow it to travel across state lines legally. I assume that these officers are on the gang's payroll." He clicked the mouse and showed Tyler one of the false records. "You can see that the officers state their full name and job title, so it should be easy for the FBI to track them down and arrest them."

This piqued Tyler's interest. "Did you see Crenshaw's name on any of these documents?"

Blade shook his head. "You think that Crenshaw might have turned to the dark side?"

"It's a possibility. The police chief's brand of cigar butts were all over the floor at the prison. And now we find out that he didn't even bother to carry out the proper checks when setting up the undercover operation." Tyler sucked air through his teeth. "I'm even starting to wonder whether Crenshaw might be Mr. X himself. Dennison said that The Scorpions' leader was a law enforcement officer."

"We should try to get this information to Dennison," Blade said. "He'll be able to pass it on to the FBI's Organized Crime Unit to investigate thoroughly. If Crenshaw's involved, Dennison has the resources to uncover it."

"Agreed," Tyler said. "Did you find anything that might prove Joanna's innocence?"

Blade rubbed his eyes. "I've uncovered zero information about Joanna, and I'm not hopeful of finding any. All of this data seems to relate only to the gang's day-to-day activities, like an instruction manual I guess."

"You look tired," Tyler said, sitting beside him. "This is great work, Blade, but you need to get some rest now. I'll take the first guard shift."

Blade pushed his coffee mug to one side. "You're right. The caffeine isn't having any effect at all."

He shifted to the edge of his seat and reached under the table for something. It was then that Tyler realized Blade had removed his prosthetic leg, and he was reaching for crutches hidden away. It was always a shock when he remembered that Blade had lost a leg, and this time was no different. Blade obviously noticed the look of surprise pass over Tyler's face.

"The residual limb sometimes gets sore, so I like to give it a rest every now and again," he said, pulling himself up to stand with the aid of the crutches. The left leg of his pants dangled down limply. "I know it must be strange for you to see me like this, but you'll get used to it."

Tyler rubbed his temples. "It's so wrong that I don't remember something as important as you losing a leg."

"Still nothing coming back, huh?"

"I'm seeing flashes of things in my mind," Tyler said. "Like shooting practice at the police training center and putting on a sheriff's hat in front of a mirror." He shook his head. "But I'm not sure if they're real memories or just my brain trying to create a backstory." He looked at Blade. "Can I ask you something?"

Blade sat back down, leaning his crutches against a chair. "Sure."

"Why did I leave the SEALs to move to a small town like Godspeed and become a sheriff? It's not exactly the most exciting place in the world, is it?"

"You were ready for the change, Tyler. You said you wanted to go back to your hometown and live a slower pace of life. You even hoped you might get married and have some kids. Every man's life goes in phases, and you'd entered the settling down phase."

Tyler laughed. "Well, that didn't quite work out for me, did it?"

"You're not even forty years old yet," Blade said. "You've got plenty of time."

"It doesn't feel that way when seven years can pass in the blink of an eye."

"Those years will come back," Blade said convincingly. "You just have to be patient and try not to force things."

"That's almost the exact same advice I gave to Joanna."

"Then it must be good. How's Joanna doing? She seemed really quiet when we got back from the prison."

"She's okay." Tyler thought of all the things he wanted to say. He wanted to tell Blade about Joanna's cancer, her fear that it would return, her belief that her life was worth less than others. He wanted to tell Blade all of this and more, knowing that the advice he would receive would be strong and true. But he couldn't betray Joanna's confidence so, instead, he said, "She's having a hard time dealing with the situation, but that's understandable. I'm trying my best to support her."

"She couldn't ask for better," Blade said, reaching for his crutches again and freezing midway. He spun his head to Tyler. "Did you see that?"

Tyler sprang up from his chair. "See what?"

"A flashlight. Outside in the trees." He pulled himself up to stand. "There it is again. Do you see it now?"

In the black woods beyond, a tiny beam of light was dancing in the branches, as though bouncing with a running man. Somebody was there. Somebody had found them.

Tyler reached for his gun at the same time as

Blade reached for his prosthesis. Both men were preparing themselves for a visit from danger.

"Don't leave the cabin," Tyler said. "Stay here and protect Joanna. I'm going outside."

SIX

Tyler ran quickly and quietly across the grass between the cabin and the woods beyond. The ground was slightly mushy and slippery with the wet snow, and he struggled to keep a sure footing. There was nothing to guide his way except for the weak moonlight, and all he could do was concentrate on the bright beam dancing through the trees, hoping to reach it before it melted away into the darkness, only to likely resurface at the cabin.

He had Joanna's assurance that she would try to stay in control of her emotions, but he knew it would be difficult for her. If she came face-to-face with an intruder, she might confront him, even if it meant losing her life in the process. He both admired and was frustrated by her in equal measure. But he was determined not to let her down, and he approached the woods with a quickened pace, tracking the light.

He pulled his weapon from its holster and

set foot on a narrow path that had been trodden through the trees. It was a trail used by visitors to the park, leading to the lake, and the light was heading away from him at a steady speed. Around the lake was even denser woodland, with evergreens providing thick foliage for cover. If someone were to set up a watch post in the trees, they could easily be undetectable to the untrained eye. And within sniper reach of the cabin. The thought was as chilling as the air around him.

He decided to cut through the trees and try to head off the guy. The ground was rocky and unsteady, but Tyler bounced on his toes, giving him a better footing. In no time, he was ahead of the man and could see his shape more clearly. Dressed head to toe in black Lycra, he ran while wearing a headlamp, a rucksack bobbing on his back.

Tyler leaped out from the cover of the trees and raised his weapon. "Stop right there."

The man didn't even acknowledge him and changed direction, darting like a slick fish in clear water, heading on another path that forked to the right.

Tyler yelled again. "Police! Stop and raise your hands."

There was no response, and the light continued to bob and weave among the thick trunks.

Gritting his teeth, Tyler holstered his gun and took off running, arms pumping rhythmically.

In a matter of seconds, he was right behind the man, hurling himself on top of him, tackling him to the ground. The man bucked and shouted, kicking with his legs. Tyler struggled to keep a tight hold of him in the darkness.

"Get off me," the man yelled.

"What are you doing here?" Tyler demanded, managing to secure an armlock around the man's back. "Who sent you?"

"Nobody sent me," he replied, panting heavily. "I'm jogging. What do you think I'm doing?"

Tyler kept the armlock secured. "At this time? Who jogs at midnight?"

The man stopped struggling, realizing that his efforts to fight were futile. "I do," he said. "I can't sleep, so sometimes I run." The headlamp on its band began to slip down his face. "I didn't expect to be attacked by some crazy guy."

Tyler hauled the jogger to his feet and loosened his grip, allowing the man to reposition the headlamp on his blond curly hair.

"I'm a law enforcement officer," Tyler said. "Why didn't you respond to my order to stop?"

"I was listening to my iPod. I didn't hear a thing." The man angled his headlamp to search the ground, the beam finding a small black device nestled among a pile of snow-topped leaves.

"The earphones came out when you threw me to the ground. I hope it's not broken because I'd expect you to replace it."

Tyler released the man fully, accepting that he had made a terrible mistake.

"What exactly did you think I was up to anyway?" the man asked, bending to pick up his iPod. "Has somebody reported a snooper or something?" He looked Tyler up and down. "And why aren't you wearing a uniform?"

"I'm off duty," Tyler replied. "I thought you might be looking for empty properties to burglarize."

The jogger narrowed his eyes. "You're off duty, huh? Then you won't mind if I ask to see some ID."

Tyler clenched his jaw. He couldn't show this man his sheriff's ID badge. He was a wanted man.

He patted down his pockets. "I don't have it on me I'm afraid. I left it back at my cabin."

The young man's expression grew even more guarded. "So if you tell me your name, I'll check it with your station in the morning."

"Sir," Tyler said, putting some distance between them, "I'm very sorry for mistaking your jogging for an illegal activity. I hope you understand that I'm simply doing my job by trying to protect members of the public."

The man brushed himself down. "Yeah, I get it. Thankfully, my iPod is fine, but you forgot to tell me your name."

Tyler began to back away a little more. "Have a pleasant evening sir. I hope you—" He stopped midsentence. A high-pitched scream cut through the air, not too loud but clearly an expression of shock. He knew it was Joanna.

"I gotta go."

He turned and ran, hearing the guy's voice call out behind him. "Be more careful next time."

It was advice that he intended to heed.

Joanna was angry with herself for reacting in such an uncontrolled way. She had woken on the couch just a few minutes previously, groggy and disoriented. After remembering where she was, she had risen and padded into the kitchen to fill a glass with water, only to be thrown totally off guard by a figure darting past the window. She dropped the glass to the tiled floor and cried out in surprise. The suddenness of the movement had caused the knee-jerk reaction, and she had composed herself within seconds, but not before Blade came rushing in from the front porch, weapon drawn.

"What is it?" he asked, flattening his back against the window to peer out back. "Did you see something?"

"I saw a man go past the window," she said, reaching for her own weapon holstered around her waist. "I'm sorry, I didn't mean to scream." She had told Tyler she would be more careful in the future, and she had blown it already. "Where's Tyler?"

Blade headed for the back door. "We saw a flashlight in the woods. He's gone to check it out. He told me to stay here and protect you."

Joanna snorted. "I think it's more of a case of me protecting you."

Blade pulled the gingham drape to one side. "I may only have one leg, Joanna, but I can assure you that I'm as tough as any able-bodied man."

Joanna clenched her teeth, feeling ashamed. She had engaged her mouth before her brain. "I'm sorry. That was a stupid thing to say. It's just that I know I can look after myself."

"It doesn't matter," Blade said. "We've got bigger things to worry about right now." He reached out and flipped down the light switch, plunging the kitchen into darkness. "I see somebody out there," he whispered. "It's a small guy, definitely not Tyler."

Joanna suppressed the urge to go rushing out onto the deck to confront the danger with the barrel of her gun. Instead, she quickly went to Blade's side and flattened her back against the wall next to him.

"Do you think Tyler's okay?" she whispered, as a kernel of worry planted itself in her belly. "Has he been gone long?"

"I'm sure he's fine. He wouldn't want me to compromise your safety by going out looking for him."

Joanna closed her eyes. It should be *her* out there investigating the threat. It should be *her* putting her life on the line. Tyler was a healthy man with way too much to lose.

"I could go look for him while you stay and deal with the intruder," Joanna said, watching the silhouette of the man peer in through the kitchen window. "He might be in trouble."

"No. Tyler was very clear about us both remaining at the cabin."

The man began to inch slowly toward the door, hood pulled up over his face. With his hands shoved into deep pockets, there was no way of telling whether he had a weapon, but the feeling of anxiety swirling in Joanna's chest stirred up a familiar eagerness to rush headlong into action.

No, she thought. *You can't place others in jeopardy. Not again.*

"I see Tyler," Blade said, reaching for the door handle and flinging it wide open. "He's walking right into this guy's path. We have to act now."

Joanna followed Blade's lead, dashing onto the deck and raising their weapons. She saw Tyler spring up the porch steps and jump onto the veranda that skirted the cabin. He was ruddy faced and sweating, as if he had been sprinting to reach her. He saw the intruder and jerked up his gun. Now the man faced Blade and Joanna on one side and Tyler on the other. He was trapped.

"Hands where I can see them," Tyler ordered. "And show us your face."

The man removed his hands from his pockets and slowly raised them, gripping the edges of his hood and lowering it from his head.

Joanna recognized the grayish skin and discolored teeth as soon as she saw them.

"Tommy!" she exclaimed, lowering her weapon. "What are you doing here? How did you find us?"

"Agent Dennison sent me," he replied, shivering slightly in the cold night air. "He wanted me to deliver a message."

Tyler kept his gun raised. "How did he know we were here?"

"He reckoned that some of your military contacts were helping to shield you, so he did some digging. This cabin was requisitioned by an old SEAL buddy of yours a couple of days ago." Tommy smiled, showing his pale, receding gum line. "So he put two and two together and figured you'd be here."

Tyler holstered his weapon and exchanged glances with Blade. "I'm not too pleased we were that easy to find, but I guess nowhere is foolproof."

He then turned his attention to Tommy. "You can't just turn up out of the blue like this. How did you get here? Anybody could've followed you."

Tommy shook his head. "No. I'm real careful. I have to be. If The Scorpions find out I'm passing information to the FBI, they'd shoot me dead. I drove here, but I parked in the main visitor's lot and walked the rest of the way." He looked up at the cabin. "It's a secluded spot you got here. Perfect."

"It's not as perfect as it used to be," Tyler said, ushering Tommy toward the door and leading him into the kitchen.

He pulled out a chair from around the table for Tommy to sit, while Joanna locked the back door and turned to stand guard. Far from being disappointed that they had been located, she was relieved to know there was a chance others would soon follow. At least she wouldn't be stuck in this remote place, bored out of her mind. If The Scorpions came, she would give them the fight of their lives.

"What did Agent Dennison want to tell us?" Tyler asked, sitting next to Tommy. Blade positioned himself on the other side, clearly still wary of this unannounced visitor.

Tommy reached into the back pocket of his jeans and pulled out some photographs, placing them on the table and smoothing out the creases with his fingertips. Then he spread them out in a line. Each photo showed a portly police officer in uniform. In some pictures, he was standing next to a Daily Delivery courier vehicle outside the old prison and in others he was walking alongside armed men through the prison entrance.

The figure was recognizable to all of them, but Joanna was the first to say his name out loud. "It's Chief Crenshaw."

"That's him," Tommy said. "Crenshaw's been having a lot of meetings with top ranking gang members over the last few days. Agent Dennison's been trying to find out exactly what his role in The Scorpions is, but it's hard to get information without attracting suspicion. The rumor in crack houses is that Godspeed's police chief is getting rich from The Scorpions. He just bought himself a nice, expensive new car."

"Yeah, he did," Joanna chimed in. "But he said he was left some money in a relative's will."

Tyler picked up one of the photos and studied it. "Who took these photographs? Was it Dennison?"

"That's what he told me," Tommy replied. "He said he risked his life to take them just a couple of days ago."

Tyler rubbed his index finger over a patch of stubble on his chin. "If these pictures are genuine, then this gives me even more reason to suspect that Crenshaw is Mr. X. He should be arrested and questioned as soon as possible."

Blade then spoke up. "Surely Agent Dennison is the best person to arrange that? He's with the FBI." He looked at Tommy with narrow-eyed suspicion. "Why did Dennison send you all the way to Tennessee with this information when he could've given it to us earlier?"

"He was going to give the pictures to his handler at their next meet, but he might not get the chance now," Tommy replied. "The Scorpions put Agent Dennison under surveillance this afternoon. He called me soon after he dropped me off to say that he was being tailed by The Dentist. He thinks his cover has been blown."

Joanna was instantly concerned, especially with mention of The Dentist. "Well, he needs to get out of Godspeed. Now."

Tommy fidgeted with his grubby fingernails as he spoke. "Yeah, yeah, he knows. He said he was gonna call his FBI handler and request an immediate pull out. But he's worried that it might be too late." Tommy cast his eyes down to his hands. "He thought he might end up dead before anybody had a chance to see these photos, so he told me where to find them and asked me to bring them to you."

"Why not give them to his handler?" Tyler suggested.

"He specifically asked me to take them to you," Tommy replied. "He seems to think that you and Deputy Graham are good, honest cops. He wanted you to have this evidence before anybody else."

"Well, he's right about Tyler and Joanna being good cops," Blade said. "But there are warrants out for their arrest. If they bring this evidence to the authorities, they'll be arrested."

Joanna wanted to take immediate action. "But if we can get Crenshaw arrested, we'll be able to prove that he framed me in order to hide his own criminal activity in the gang."

"Exactly," Tommy said with a snap of his fingers. "That's what Dennison said. He wants me to take you to an FBI safe house someplace close to Memphis tonight. He says that a team of federal agents are based there. You'll be safe while you decide who to trust with this evidence."

Blade looked unsure. "Why didn't he arrange all of this with us earlier? If he'd wanted to help us get into protective custody, that would have been the perfect moment."

"He wanted to check out your story first," Tommy replied. "He made some calls, found out that you guys are decent people and decided to work with you."

Blade's facial expression didn't change. "Well, I don't think any of us want to go with you to Memphis without checking it out first," he said, looking at Tyler, who nodded in agreement.

"But I gotta take you guys to the safe house," Tommy said, his voice rising to a whine. "I promised Dennison I would. They're expecting us."

Joanna looked across at Tyler and Blade. "This is our best chance of exposing Crenshaw and proving my innocence. We should go to Memphis with Tommy right away."

Neither man spoke for a few seconds. It was Blade who broke the silence with just one word. "No."

Tyler appeared thoughtful, his eyes running over the photographs on the table. "I agree. I'd rather not go anywhere unless I know exactly who's there waiting for me. I strongly suspect that Crenshaw is involved with The Scorpions, but we haven't had these photos verified as authentic." He held one up to the overhead light. "The shadows look all wrong on this one. It might have been Photoshopped."

Joanna took the picture from his hands. "It looks perfectly legitimate to me." She tried to hide her rising impatience. She thought Tyler was trying to find problems where there were none.

"We can't just sit on this evidence. We should act immediately."

"That's precisely what we shouldn't do," Tyler said. "Only fools rush in."

"So what do you suggest, Sheriff?" she asked, her voice taking on a sarcastic tone. She was annoyed by the inference that she was a fool.

"I suggest," he said, standing, "that we do nothing until tomorrow." He put a hand on Tommy's shoulder. "You'll stay with us for the night, and we'll make a plan of action in the morning."

Tommy's face looked momentarily panicked. "But Agent Dennison wanted us to leave tonight. I don't want to let him down."

Tyler was unmoved by the plea. "I'm sorry, Tommy, but we don't know you well enough to trust you on this. You're a virtual stranger to us."

A crestfallen look passed over Tommy's face, and Joanna's hackles rose.

"That's unfair," she protested. "I'm a virtual stranger to you, too, but you made a decision to trust me."

The silence that followed caused Joanna's belly to go into free fall. "You *do* trust me, don't you, Tyler?"

"Of course I do," he said quickly, but it was too late. She saw the doubt on his face. He couldn't hide it.

"Can I ask you to hand over any electronic devices like a cell phone or tablet?" Blade asked, patting down Tommy's pockets. "It's just a precaution. These devices can be tracked." He slipped a cell from the informant's jacket. "You can have it back when you leave."

Tommy stood. "I should go," he said. He was jittery. "I don't want to put you guys in danger. I'll head back to Godspeed and tell Dennison that you'd rather not get involved."

Tyler put a hand on Tommy's shoulder. "We never said that we didn't want to get involved. We'll make sure these photographs end up in the right hands. There's no way you should drive back to Godspeed tonight." He peered out the window to see snow falling in thick flakes. "It's not safe. Blade will show you where you can sleep."

With that, Blade took Tommy's arm and steered him from the kitchen. Joanna noticed Dennison's informant pull a cross on a chain from his shirt as he walked down the hallway. He then turned and smiled weakly at her, mouthing "thanks for trying." She smiled back, but she felt ashamed. Even a hopeless meth addict seemed to have more faith in God than she did. She was angry with Tyler for not trusting this man, simply because he was an unwashed, dirty addict. It was unjust.

"We may have just lost our only chance to

expose Crenshaw as Mr. X," she said, refusing to look Tyler in the eye. "I know you don't trust Tommy, but it's hard to accept that you don't trust *me*."

"I trust you completely," he said strongly. "But I don't know if you can trust yourself."

"What's that even supposed to mean?" she challenged.

"You still want to rush ahead on everything," he replied. "No matter how much you try to rein in the instinct, it's too ingrained in you. Your motives are honorable, but you just can't trust yourself to make good choices."

She threw back her head. "That's ridiculous. Going to Memphis with Tommy *is* a good choice."

Tyler spoke quietly. "I happen to think that you're wrong."

"No surprises there," she said derisively. "You've always thought everything I do is wrong."

"That's not true," he protested.

"What would you know?" she said, raising her voice. "You don't remember anything about me." She turned on her heel, determined not to let Tyler upset her even further. "I'm going to bed. Wake me up when it's my guard shift."

"Joanna," he called, "let's not end our conversation like this."

She didn't see the point in replying.

* * *

Tyler listened to Joanna walking heavily around her room. She was angry. Earlier that morning the three friends had discussed the possibility of traveling to the safe house in Memphis, before voting on the plan. Joanna had been defeated by two votes to one. They would remain in the cabin for the foreseeable future.

Tyler's concern for Joanna's well-being was growing, and he wished he could get her to a doctor. She needed a full medical check-up as soon as possible. If her cancer had returned, she would need to start on a program of treatment.

He rubbed a hand across his chest. He had been trying very hard to keep his anxieties to himself, but he was struggling to deal with his memory loss. He had come to rely on Joanna's reassuring presence more than she could ever know. Despite his frustration with her eager and headstrong attitude, he saw something special behind her bravado, and he didn't want to fight with her. She had become his rock in many ways, the only person anchoring him to Yardley County and Godspeed. He needed her, yet she had no idea how much.

He closed his eyes and muttered a quick prayer, knowing that it was his only defense against the difficulties they were all facing.

"Nice thinking," Blade said, entering the front

door and coming to sit on the couch. "Start every day with a prayer and you can't go wrong."

Tyler opened his eyes. "Where's Tommy?"

"When I told him that we wouldn't be going to Memphis with him, he decided to leave. I took him back to his car in the lot." Blade rubbed his chin. "I reckon he's the biggest coward I ever met. He's shaking like a leaf. I told him to go home, lie low and leave the investigation to us."

"The question we have to answer now," said Tyler, "is where do we go from here?"

"Before we move on to that," Blade said, "I should tell you that I dusted the piece of glass you picked up at the prison, and I found two sets of prints. Good ones, too. Really great quality. One set must be yours, but the other probably belongs to your attacker."

"That's fantastic," Tyler said, glad of the good news. "So let's remotely hack into the FBI fingerprint database and try to find a match."

Blade shook his head. "I already tried, but there's no way I can get past the firewall. The only way to run these prints would be to use a police computer that has portal access."

Tyler sighed. Maybe this good news wasn't so good after all. "I wonder if my sheriff's department has a computer with access," he said. "Joanna will know."

"What if the prints don't match up to anybody?" Blade asked. "This guy might not be on the police radar."

"That's a possibility," Tyler replied. "But plenty of The Scorpions' members will have rap sheets. We also know that they've recruited corrupt officers to the gang, and most states require police officers to submit prints on application, including Missouri."

"Are you expecting one set of prints to belong to Crenshaw?"

"I don't want to make any rash assumptions without getting Dennison's photographs analyzed," Tyler said. "But Crenshaw is my number one suspect right now."

"These prints are definitely a great lead," Blade said. "But even if the sheriff's department does have a computer with portal access, we still need an authorized login. I'm guessing you don't remember if you have one."

"Exactly right. This is where we really need Joanna's help." The photographs of Chief Crenshaw were lying on the coffee table, and Tyler reached down to pick them up. "Not only do we need to gain access to the FBI database, we should also pass these pictures along to somebody in authority as soon as possible."

"And who do you suggest?" Blade asked.

"That's the problem," Tyler replied, rubbing

the back of his neck. "I just don't remember who I can trust."

Blade put his fingertips on his temples. "Still in the dark, huh?"

"Apart from the occasional flash of memory that I can't place, I'm no better."

"It's strange," Blade said. "But you and Joanna seem to know each other so well that I can't believe you don't remember her. You act like an old married couple sometimes, especially with the bickering."

"What can I say?" he said with a laugh. "She pushes all my buttons."

"Is she okay?" Blade asked. "She seemed a little upset yesterday."

Tyler still didn't want to divulge too many personal details. "She's got a lot on her mind, and I'd like to take her back to Godspeed as soon as possible." He took a deep breath. "She's got some health issues that need to be dealt with."

Blade nodded slowly. "I understand. You're very protective of this woman, Tyler. I don't think I've seen you this way before."

Tyler was surprised. "Don't read too much into it. I'm just trying to keep her safe."

"Hey," said Blade with a wave of his hand. "I'm not reading anything into it. I just wanted to check that you know what you're doing."

Tyler felt himself becoming a little defensive.

"Of course I know what I'm doing. I'm trying to help my deputy prove her innocence."

Blade shifted position and came to sit closer. "I know you *feel* like you know Joanna," he said quietly. "But you don't. Everybody you met in the last seven years is a stranger to you. And that includes her."

Tyler read between the lines. "Are you telling me that you don't trust her?"

Blade smiled wryly. "I don't trust anybody until I've jumped out of an airplane with them and parachuted smack bang in the middle of enemy territory. I can count the number of people I truly trust on one hand. Don't get me wrong, I like Joanna. She's brave and tough, that's for sure, but neither of us really knows her."

Tyler opened his mouth to protest, but he closed it again. Technically, Blade was right.

"I've noticed an intimacy between the two of you, although you cover it up with arguments," Blade continued. "And it worries me a little."

"It does?"

"Of course. You guys already tried dating once and it didn't work out. I don't want to see you walk down the same road and end up in the same place. I'm just looking out for you, buddy. Don't get too close."

"Thanks for the advice," Tyler said dismissively. "But I'm definitely not getting too close.

Joanna and I are like oil and water. You don't need to worry."

Blade leaned back in his chair. "Don't I? Sometimes a beautiful woman can make a man lose his sense of judgment."

Tyler shook his head. "I may have lost several years of my life, but my judgment remains as solid as ever. I'm not going to get romantically involved with Joanna. I'd be playing with fire."

Joanna's voice floated through the air as she breezed into the living room, catching the end of their conversation.

"Who's playing with fire?" she asked, perching on the edge of the couch, freshly showered and wearing jeans and a hooded sweatshirt. It seemed like she had burned off all her earlier anger and was now more relaxed. "Since we decided not to go to Memphis, what's the new plan for today?"

An awkward silence descended over the room before Tyler spoke. "Blade lifted some prints from the glass we found at the prison. We now need to find a computer with portal access to the FBI fingerprint database."

"There's one at the sheriff's department in Godspeed," she said. "I've used it a few times."

"So you know the access details?" Tyler asked hopefully.

"Sure. If you can get me to the office, I can log us in."

"We'll have to break in overnight," he said. "We can't run the risk of being seen." He held up the photographs. "We also need to pass along these pictures to somebody trustworthy in law enforcement. Do you have any suggestions?"

Joanna answered instantly. "What about Luke?"

Tyler cocked his head to the side. The name sounded familiar, but he didn't know why. It was a feeling he should be used to by now. "Who's Luke?"

"You have two deputies," Joanna replied. "I'm one, and the other is Luke Hutchence. He's been a Yardley deputy for almost twenty years, and I'm certain that he'd do the right thing with this information. He's about as good and honest as they come."

"How come you never mentioned his name before now?"

Joanna shrugged. "You didn't ask."

Tyler exchanged a fleeting look with Blade that was loaded with meaning. The old SEAL comrades were both in the dark where Yardley County was concerned, and Joanna was their only reference point. Luke's name had never been mentioned before, and for a split second Tyler wondered whether this mysterious second deputy truly existed.

Don't be stupid, he thought. *You can trust this woman.*

"Okay," Tyler said. "How do we get in touch with him?"

Joanna grabbed a pad and pen from the table. "I'll write his contact details here."

As she scribbled on the paper, Tyler's belly tied itself into a knot. Until this moment, he'd felt certain of Joanna's honesty. But Blade's questioning had planted a seed of doubt that he knew would be difficult to uproot.

Was Joanna as honest as he'd assumed?

SEVEN

Joanna watched Blade set up a mass of cables and wires around his laptop on the kitchen table, connecting them to small devices, blinking with lights. She felt a sense of unease hanging in the air. When she had walked in on Tyler and Blade's earlier conversation, she'd been sure they had been discussing her. Something about the expression on their faces reminded her of children being caught stealing candy: guilty.

"Are you sure that emailing Luke is the best way of contacting him?" Joanna asked, walking to the coffeepot and pouring herself a large mug. "There must be a quicker way."

"Sometimes speed isn't everything," Blade replied, tapping away on the keyboard. "If we telephone him from a landline, the police will instantly try to trace the number. If we use a cell phone, the provider may be able to give them our geographical location. But if the police try to trace our email, it will lead them all over the world, thanks to a very careful setup that reroutes our proxy server wherever we want it to go. I just have to set up an untraceable email address and we're good to go."

Joanna surveyed the mass of wiring. Her exasperation was growing, and she swallowed it. Luke might not respond to an email for hours. They could be stuck there, twiddling their thumbs until the evening. Tomorrow was Christmas Eve. She had hoped they would able to return to Godspeed for the holidays, but she had clearly been kidding herself.

Tyler, standing close by, guessed how she was feeling and put his hand on the small of her back, leading her into the living room.

"I know you want to move quickly on this, but we need to be really cautious about how we proceed."

Joanna sighed. "But there must be a quicker method than email."

"There isn't," Tyler said. "Let's trust Blade on this. He's a communications expert. He'll cover our tracks so well that no one will have a clue where we are."

Joanna raised her eyes to the ceiling. Her shoulders were tense and her neck was stiff. The soreness in her armpit had dulled to a mild throb, and a swelling had popped up, soft and squishy with the yellowing marks of tissue damage. It must be a bruise. She kept telling herself this over and over. It must be a bruise.

"How's the pain you were telling me about yesterday?" Tyler asked, putting a tentative hand on her shoulder.

His blue eyes were slightly moist and his baby face didn't look quite so young today. He had grown stubble, faintly flecked with gray, hiding his dimples, and the effect was to make him appear more rugged. Joanna took a deep breath, suppressing a fluttering heart. Her attraction to the sheriff had never been a problem. She had always covered it up with a professional and go-getting attitude. In fact, her job provided a mask for a whole lot of emotions.

"It's okay," she lied. "I was just being paranoid." She looked away. "It's fine."

He put his fingers on the side of her head and gently steered her face back toward his. "Joanna." The tone of his voice told her that he wasn't buying it. "If we're going to be working closely together during this investigation, I don't want you to lie to me. I'm here to support you. Talk to me."

She squeezed her eyes shut. The last thing she wanted to do was talk to Tyler. She'd already opened up to him once, and once was enough.

She opened her eyes but kept them downcast. "It was just a false alarm."

He took his hand from her cheek. "So there's no pain?"

"No."

He didn't look convinced. "Would you like to see a doctor today anyway?"

She shook her head quickly. "No, definitely not."

"But it might put your mind at rest."

"It would place us all in danger," she said. "And you reminded me that I'm not supposed to do that anymore."

Tyler gave a sigh of frustration. "That's not what I meant, and you know it."

Joanna wrapped her arms around herself, holding her coffee mug next to the swelling, where the warming discomfort added to her anxiety. She knew that the position of this inflammation was where her lymph nodes were located. If the tumor was back, it could have spread to her lymphatic system without her knowing. And beyond.

"It's just a tiny bruise," she said. "Let's not make a big fuss about it."

Tyler rubbed his forehead as if carefully considering what to say next.

"Take a seat," he said, sitting on the couch. "Blade will be a while setting up in the kitchen, so let's talk."

Joanna shrugged. "I thought we just did."

He laughed. "If that's what you call talking, then you need to work on your conversational skills."

Joanna reluctantly sat on the couch next to him, placing her mug on the table.

Tyler took her hands in his. "I want you to be able to share anything with me," he said. "I get the feeling you're trying to downplay your fears. If you'd like to visit a local doctor and get checked over, then I'm happy to find one for you. Your health is more important than any investigation."

She swallowed a knot that was forming in her throat. She *did* want to see a doctor, but at the same time she didn't. What she wanted much more was to get on with the task of exposing Crenshaw as their likely Mr. X.

"I don't want to see a doctor," she said flatly. "Now can we change the subject, please?"

"Sure."

"What about you?" she asked, turning the tables on him. "How are you feeling? We shouldn't forget that you suffered a nasty trauma recently, too."

He twisted his body on the couch to face her. "I'm doing okay, but I'd like to discuss Godspeed and fill in a couple more gaps."

She was relieved. This was a nice safe subject. "Sure. What do you want to know?"

"Why don't we start with Luke?" he said. "Tell me more about him."

"Luke was a police officer in St. Louis before relocating to Yardley County. He wanted to move his family to a small rural town like Godspeed. He's a stickler for rules." She laughed. "So it goes without saying that you two get along really well. Like I said before, he's a good, honest man, the kind of old-school cop that everybody loves."

She noticed Tyler watching her intently, hanging on her every word. "Like I said, it's funny that you never mentioned him before."

Did she see a flash of mistrust in his eyes? "I saw no reason to mention him before now," she said. "I wasn't withholding information deliberately." She narrowed her eyes. "Are you saying that you don't believe me?"

Tyler was quick to respond. "No, not at all."

Then she saw where the suspicion truly came from. "But Blade's not so sure about me, right?"

"Blade quite rightly pointed out to me that neither of us really knows you."

Joanna felt an ache in her heart. She had known Tyler for three years, and yet he clearly knew nothing about her character. Nothing at all.

Tyler continued. "So this is why I need to ensure that you're always honest with me, Joanna. When you're not truthful, it makes me wonder what else you might have lied about."

She snatched her hands away from his. "I *am* truthful," she protested. "You're the very last person in the world I would want to deceive, Tyler. I know we've often clashed in the past, but I would never lie to you."

He dropped his voice low. "But you lied to me just a few minutes ago."

Joanna took a deep breath to dispute his words when she realized that he was right. She *had* lied to him. She had done it to protect him, or to protect herself. She wasn't quite sure, but either way, it wasn't the right thing to do.

She lifted her right arm and put her palm over the painful area. "I have a small swelling here that's very tender to the touch. After my cancer diagnosis, I underwent two full mastectomies to try to stop the tumor from growing back, but cancer cells can travel around the body. The most likely place I'm going to grow any new tumors is right here in my armpit." She stopped to take a steadying breath. Being truthful was a lot harder than Tyler appreciated. "It would mean that the cancer is in my lymphatic system. It could be anywhere by now. My lungs, liver, blood, brain..." She tailed off. Tyler wanted honesty, and she had given him honesty, warts and all.

"You said that you fell against a wall yesterday chasing Tommy in the prison, right?" Tyler said. "That's probably the cause of the tenderness. In my experience, the most likely explanation is usually the correct one."

"That's what I've been telling myself," she said, repeating the mantra of the last few hours. "It's just a bruise."

"But that doesn't stop you from being scared."

She folded her arms. "I'm not scared."

His eyes softened. She knew he saw through her. What was the point in pretending anymore?

"Okay, yes, I'm scared," she admitted. "I'm terrified that my life plans will come to nothing. I might never get the chance to marry a man I love, have a family or retire to a cabin in the mountains where I can have my own vegetable garden. I'm afraid that my parents will have to buy a casket for me and put me in the ground." She clenched her fingers tight. "I don't want to be denied all these basic things that everybody else takes for granted. I don't want to die before making my mark on the world."

She allowed Tyler to take her hands again. "Trust me, Joanna, you've already made your mark on the world. You've certainly made your mark on me." He leaned forward, bringing his face close to hers. His breath was minty, and his scent was woody. "You can't control what the future holds, and I want you to stop being afraid."

She couldn't help but let out a high-pitched laugh. "That's easy for you to say."

"Actually," he said. "It isn't easy at all. Since I lost my memory, I've been living in a world of unknowns. Sometimes I don't have a clue who I am or why I'm here. I look in the mirror and see a man I hardly recognize. My best friend lost a leg, and I don't even remember it happening. But worst of all, I dated a woman as amazing as you, and I can't recall any of the times we spent together. Even if we're not a good match, we must have made sparks fly." He took a deep breath. "So please trust me when I say that I know how it feels to be afraid. I have to learn how to live my life all over again, and it's pretty terrifying. But we can get through this together if we both make the choice not to be scared."

Joanna was temporarily stunned into silence. Did Tyler just call her an amazing woman? Could she have possibly heard him right? She had no idea that he saw her that way. She was the wild card, the nuisance, the maverick. Yes, they definitely made sparks fly, but ultimately she drove him crazy.

She squeezed his fingers. "I want to make that choice with you, Tyler. I want to stop being afraid, but it's not that easy."

"I know that," he said gently. "That's why I want you to let me support you. If the pain worsens or you decide you need to see a doctor, tell me. Promise me you'll do that."

She found it hard to make that promise, but she knew it was right. "I promise." The knot in her throat worked its way upward. "Thank you, Tyler. I appreciate your care of me."

He smiled. "I'm glad you've been honest with me. From now on, we have no secrets, okay?"

Neither said anything for a few seconds, and Joanna felt the old electricity fizzing between them. She searched his face, and he leaned in even closer. She saw his blue-gray eyes come into sharp focus.

Just as their lips were about to touch, Blade strode into the room, and they jumped apart like coiled springs.

"Our email account is up and running," Blade said, failing to notice the moment he had interrupted. "Let's do this thing."

Tyler reread his carefully worded email message for the third time:

Deputy Hutchence,
I need your help. I would like to meet with you as soon as possible regarding the handover of vital evidence relating to The Scorpions investigation. You must come alone. Please do not inform anybody else of this message. I hope we

can trust you. I urge you not to believe what you have been told about Joanna. She is innocent, and with your help we can prove it.

I am awaiting your reply,
Sheriff Tyler Beck

He hovered his finger over the mouse, knowing that once he pressed Send, the message would be irretrievable. They would have dragged Deputy Hutchence into their investigation and possibly into danger.

"Do it," Joanna urged. "What do we have to lose?"

With a glance between Joanna and Blade, Tyler clicked the mouse and watched the email vanish from the screen, winging its way to his deputy in Yardley County. Blade had set up an account with the user name *Sheriff Beck* so that Luke would instantly read the mail and respond quickly.

Tyler stood and stretched the muscles of his back. "Well, now all we have to do is wait."

He felt Joanna's hand rest on his shoulder and he saw her smile at him. She seemed a lot more relaxed since their recent conversation, and he was acutely aware that there was an increasing closeness between them. Blade had called him out on it already. When Joanna was calm and still, he was drawn to her like a moth to a flame, but how long would her newfound tranquility last? He had to accept that people could not change overnight, and he knew there was a long road ahead. He hadn't been thinking straight when he had leaned in to kiss her. He'd been foolish to think they could overcome their differences in just one conversation.

"I don't think Luke will let us down," Joanna said, returning his wandering thoughts back into the room.

Then, as if her words were a portent, a ping came from the computer, and Blade looked sharply at the screen.

"That's the noise I rigged to let us know that an email has been received," he said, grabbing the computer mouse. "It's Luke. He replied already. Wow that was quick."

Tyler sat back down and read the reply out loud: "'I'll do anything I can to help you, Sheriff. Just name the time and the place and I'll be there. You have my loyalty. Luke.'"

Seeing Luke's words on the screen triggered a twinge of familiarity in Tyler. In his mind he saw his two deputies, in uniform, in an open plan office, laughing and joking next to a large window, under which stood a water cooler. He was certain that he was seeing the sheriff's department. And it gave him a sensation of warmth and comfort.

For the first time since his memory loss, he felt a pang of homesickness, not for Little Creek, Virginia, but for Godspeed.

Before suggesting a location, Tyler tapped out a question:

What's going on there, Deputy?

Blade and Joanna looked to be holding their breath waiting for Luke's reply to come through. When it did, Tyler read it to them. "'The county commissioner is arranging the appointment of a temporary sheriff, but Chief Crenshaw is poking his nose into the sheriff's department's business in the meantime. He's going nuts trying to find you guys. He makes appeals on the news stations every day. He thinks you've gone out of state, and he's asked the police in Arkansas, Tennessee and Kentucky to keep a lookout for you. I'm not sure it's safe for you to come out of hiding.'"

Tyler wanted to choose a meeting place that both he and Luke would know, a wide open space with visibility for miles around.

I'll take that risk. Can you meet me at the old prison at 8:00 p.m. tonight? It's vital that you come alone.

The reply was almost instant:

I'll be there alone.

Tyler tapped one final message:

Keep this line of communication open today. We'll do the same.

Sure thing. Stay safe, Sheriff.

Tyler then checked his watch. "It should only take me a couple of hours to get to the old prison from here," he said. "But I can't take the motorcycle. It's too visible." He looked over at Blade. "Can I borrow your truck?"

Blade looked confused. "Sure, but aren't we all going?"

Tyler hadn't considered this option. "I figured that you'd stay here with Joanna."

Joanna crossed her arms. "Why?" Her tone was defensive.

He rubbed a hand down his face guessing that this would be tricky. "It makes sense for you to stay hidden. If something happens and I'm attacked or arrested, then at least you won't be placed in danger, as well."

"So why don't I go instead of you?" she said.

"It's me who's put us in this position, and it's me who should take the risk."

Tyler sighed. Not this again. So much for her newfound tranquility.

"You have too much to lose," he said. "If you're arrested, you'll probably be categorized as a flight risk and denied bail."

"It's no different for you," she said with a shake of her head. "You'd be denied bail, too."

"Yes, but…" He stopped. He didn't want to complete the sentence.

"But what?" she challenged. "You can talk openly in front of Blade. I don't mind."

He stood to face her. "If I'm arrested, I won't be stuck in a jail cell worrying about my health. Or worse, be taken to the hospital for medical treatment under armed guard." He took a step closer to her, and she took a step back. Blade quietly left the room. "I know that your swelling is probably nothing more than a bruise," he said, "but I want to be cautious. I want you to be able to walk into a doctor's office without cuffs on your wrists."

She eyeballed him, unblinking. "I'm coming to Godspeed with you."

He sighed. "I can't allow it."

Her eyebrows shot up high. "You can't allow it? Who do you think you are?"

"I'm your sheriff, Deputy Graham."

She threw back her head and laughed. "How can you be my sheriff when you don't even remember being sworn in? Admit it—you don't actually want to be the sheriff, do you? You want to go back to the SEALs and leave us all behind, so quit acting the hero."

Tyler fell silent, and Joanna brought her hands up to her face as if the force of her aggression had taken even her by surprise.

"I'm sorry, Tyler," she said. "That was totally uncalled for." She sat heavily in a chair. "I lost my cool."

He sat next to her. He had encouraged her to be completely honest with him and had reaped what he'd sown. And now he had to be as candid with her as she'd been with him.

"It's okay," he said, watching her bend her head to let silken strands of hair obscure her face. "When I found out that I was the sheriff of Yardley County, I was thrown for a loop. And you're right—I wanted to be back with my SEAL unit in Virginia. I never imagined myself being the sheriff of a rural county, living in a small town, watching tumbleweeds pass by."

Joanna looked up. Her eyes were red-rimmed, but they were burning fiercely. "Yardley County is full of good, decent people who are proud of all they've achieved. Last year, you cut the ribbon to open a new community hall, built entirely with public donations. I'm sure that the SEALs don't build any community halls, or sport centers or libraries…" She tailed off and wiped beneath her eyes with her sleeve. "You make us Yardley folk sound like a bunch of hicks, and it's offensive."

"I know," he said quietly. He deserved the rebuke and took it humbly. "I see that now. I didn't give Yardley a chance. When I was a younger man, I couldn't wait to leave Godspeed behind and head out into the big, wide world. Now that I've suddenly found myself back there, I'm afraid of feeling the need to escape again. I'm sorry."

A faint smile passed her lips, giving him hope that she had forgiven him. "I thought we made a pact not to be afraid," she said.

"Yes, we did," he said, smiling back at her. "So that's why I'm embracing my role as sheriff and affirming my commitment to being the best sheriff that Yardley County has ever had."

"That won't be hard," she said, her eyes losing their ferocity and relaxing instead. "Some of the sheriffs we've had in the past have been pretty awful."

He laughed. Yes, she had forgiven him, and he was glad.

"So what do you say the two of us get back to work as soon as all of this is behind us?" he said. "There must be a lot of catching up to do."

"What about your amnesia?" she asked. "Won't you need rehabilitation treatment?"

"Perhaps," he said with a slow nod. "But I think that my memory is slowly starting to return." He recalled his earlier vision of his deputies in uniform. "Does our station have large, white-trimmed windows and a water cooler beside a leafy plant in a yellow pot?"

"Yes!" she exclaimed. "You remember it."

"I do," he said. "And the more I concentrate, the more I see." He closed his eyes. "In my mind I'm walking out the door and into the parking lot. I see my cruiser and a coffee place across the street."

"Yes," Joanna urged, clearly excited at his accuracy. "What else do you see?"

Tyler thought hard. "I see..." His vision changed. He was back in the prison, running through the deserted, derelict corridors, the stench of dampness filling his nostrils. He was racing to reach Joanna, following the sounds of gunfire. Then, in his mind, he spun around as a gunshot ricocheted off the rusted, steel bars of a nearby cell. He spoke his thoughts out loud. "I'm in the old prison. I see a man dressed in black. He's shooting at me, and I take cover in a cell, shooting back. We both run out of ammo, and he turns to flee." Tyler grimaced, desperately trying to see the man's face, but it would not come into focus, and he concluded that it had to have been covered by a mask. "I run toward him and tackle him to the ground. We fight. I land a punch, and he twists away. He picks up a rock while I'm getting to my feet. He holds the rock high in the air and swings it downward on my head." Tyler automatically brought his fingers up to the spot where his wound had been stitched. "The rock cuts me here."

"But this blow doesn't knock you out?" Joanna asked breathlessly. He opened his eyes to see that she was mesmerized by his story, staring intently at him. "What happened next?"

Tyler closed his eyes again, waiting to pick up the thread of memory. "I see a piece of glass on the ground, so I grab it and swipe at the guy. I cut his arm. A spurt of blood splatters on the wall and he cries out, but he carries on fighting with me." Tyler rested his head in his hands as the feelings of the remembered moment became stronger. "All I can think about is getting to you. You need my help, and I can't reach you. I hear your voice calling my name, and I'm distracted. I turn my head. The guy grabs the glass from my hand, and it clatters to the floor. Then I see the rock coming at me again. I put up my hand, but it's too late to stop the impact." He opened his eyes. "And then I wake up on the floor."

Joanna smiled. "This is incredible, Tyler.

These memories could prove vital in our investigation. Your brain is reconnecting itself again. How does it feel?"

"Weird," Tyler said, as a sensation of dizziness hit him. "Dr. Sinclair did say that most memory loss of this type is resolved spontaneously, but I never really expected it to happen so suddenly. It's like pieces of a puzzle are putting themselves together, but I'm not sure where all the parts go just yet."

Joanna reached out and patted his hand, much like a teacher might do with a child. He felt her uncertainty regarding how much affection to show. He felt the same way. He wanted to gather her into his arms and celebrate, but it wouldn't be right.

"Welcome back," she said. "The people of Yardley County will be pleased to know that you're still with us."

"I have a long way to go," Tyler said. "But I'm on the road at least."

"Speaking of being on the road…" she started.

He knew where this line of conversation was headed, and he accepted defeat. "If you're determined to come to Godspeed this evening, then the three of us will go together," he said. "But I'd rather you used the time to go see a doctor at the hospital. I'll call Dr. Sinclair and ask if he'd be willing to see you in secret."

To his surprise, Joanna didn't put up a fight. She touched the area under her arm. "I think that's a good idea."

"After you're done at the hospital, we'll meet up again, but if anything happens to me, you and Blade leave immediately and get back here to continue the investigation. Agreed?"

"Agreed."

Tyler rubbed his eyes. He and Joanna had managed to formulate a plan without disagreement. "That's the first time we've agreed on anything, do you know that?"

Before she had a chance to reply, a ping echoed through the air from the kitchen, letting them know that an email had been received. Tyler heard Blade's distinctive footfall in the hallway as he rushed from his bedroom to read the message.

He and Joanna sprang up from the couch and reached the computer just as Blade sat at the table.

"You'll want to see this," Blade said, turning the screen to Tyler.

It was an email from Luke. Tyler read the message aloud: "'I just heard that a meth user by the name of Tommy Roper walked into the Godspeed police station this morning and requested police protection. He says he's an informant for an undercover FBI agent in The Scorpions who has disappeared. He claims that the gang has now targeted him for elimination and he's being followed by some guy called The Dentist. The Feds are sending agents to meet with him this afternoon. Tommy is also claiming to have met with you yesterday. Is this something we should be worried about?'"

Tyler wasted no time in writing his reply:

YES. Has he revealed our location?

The reply was instant and relieving:

No. But I have a feeling that Crenshaw will crack him soon.

Tyler breathed hard, trying to work out what to do about this potentially disastrous situation.

"Why would Tommy go to the chief for help?" Blade asked disbelievingly. "If Dennison suspects that Crenshaw is Mr. X, then Tommy should be getting as far away from him as possible."

"Who knows what Tommy's game is?" Tyler said. "But he's obviously returned to Godspeed, found that Dennison has vanished and is terrified that he's next on The Scorpions' hit list. He may be working on the assumption that it's safer to keep your friends close but your enemies closer.

If Crenshaw *is* Mr. X, he'll want to keep Tommy alive long enough to find out where we're hiding. And if he talks, we're in deep trouble. We can't take that chance. We gotta leave."

Tyler quickly tapped out a reply to Luke:

Thanks for the heads-up, but our plan remains unchanged—8:00 at the prison.

Tyler then stood, palms flat on the table, thinking as fast as he could. "Let's all pack our things as quickly as possible. Leave no trace behind. I want to be ready to go in twenty minutes at the very most." He turned to Blade. "Leave this equipment here for now, and we'll pack it up at the last minute." He raked his fingers through his hair. This was a nasty surprise that they didn't need.

Blade and Joanna hurried from the room, leaving Tyler to gather his thoughts in the silence.

Was their secluded hiding spot about to be laid wide open?

Joanna rammed her belongings into her bag. She had very few items to pack, but she wanted to be sure that she followed Tyler's exact instruction and left no trace behind. It seemed so unfair to have gotten so close to unmasking Mr. X only for Tommy to go and threaten their progress. But she was comforted by the fact that Tyler was recovering his memory. It was fantastic news.

Then Joanna stopped in her tracks for a few seconds as a thought hit her. Tyler would soon recover his memories of *her*. He would remember how they bickered and argued even more frequently than they did now. Would it change the way he saw her? She felt as though she and Tyler had taken significant steps forward in their friendship. They had talked openly and honestly, giving them a closeness that they had failed to achieve before. Would that progress now crumble to dust as Tyler remembered more of their history?

She muttered to herself as she walked around her bedroom checking beneath the bed and nightstand.

"It doesn't matter," she told herself. "You and Tyler were over anyway."

She heard Blade and Tyler talking in the room next door, discussing whether to take the motorcycle or dump it along the way. They didn't hear the ping of a newly arrived email echo down the hallway.

Joanna secured the strap on her backpack and walked quickly into the kitchen, dropping the bag to the floor and turning the computer monitor to read the words.

She sprang back from the screen, a gasp of

shock escaping her lips. This setback had just gone from bad to worse in a split second.

Luke's most recent email contained just one line, written in big, bold capital letters:

POLICE ARE COMING. RUN.

EIGHT

Joanna shouted out, rushing to the living-room window to check if anybody was heading their way.

"Tyler, Blade, we need to leave. Right now."

Luke had obviously had no time to elaborate on his simple message. Maybe somebody was in the station with him, and he'd sent the stark warning hoping not to be seen. Whatever the reason, the advice was clear: get out of there.

Tyler burst into the living room, weapon drawn. "What's happened?"

Joanna raced from window to window. "Luke says police are coming. We need to go."

Blade lost no time in yanking the wires from his laptop, stuffing cables and routers into a large bag.

"Leave that equipment here," Tyler said. "The plan just changed. We only take the bare essentials."

"It's all essential," Blade said, looking up quickly. "We can't leave it behind."

Tyler grabbed the key to Blade's truck from the dresser. "You ready?"

"I'm almost done," Blade said, using a sweeping motion to drop the remaining items into the open bag. He zipped it up and walked into the living room, holding the heavy bag by his side. "Good to go."

Then, without warning, he fell to the floor, as a slicing sound zipped through the air. The window shattered, the atmosphere became surreal and Joanna froze, watching Blade clutch his arm as a seeping bloodstain spread on his plaid shirt.

She realized that Tyler was yelling out her name. "Joanna, get down!"

She let her legs buckle beneath her, and she fell hard to the wooden boards, hearing another shot zing through the air, right where she had just been standing. The bullet slammed into the wall, sending splinters spitting onto the rug. The gunfire was eerily quiet. Somebody was using a silencer to avoid attracting attention. This surely couldn't be the police. This must be a Scorpions attack.

"Blade," Tyler called out. "How bad is it?"

His voice was loud and clear in reply. "It's okay. The bullet just grazed the skin."

Joanna crawled over to the men, by the hearth, and pulled a small pack of tissues from her pocket. "Here," she said, handing them to Blade. "These might help." She lifted her head to peer out the window. "I have no idea where this shooter is."

Tyler pushed her shoulder downward to take her out of the line of fire. "It's not one shooter. It's two."

Joanna tried to shield her head as glass rained down on them from a mirror above the fireplace that shattered into hundreds of pieces as the gunfire intensified.

"Are you sure?" she asked.

"Yes. I think that one guy is in the woods using a sniper rifle, and the other is close by with a handgun with a silencer." As if to prove his point, two shots rang out, both rounds almost hitting the same spot—the shattered mirror frame above their heads.

"They're trying to drive us outside," Blade said. "We don't stand a chance against a good sniper. The truck is parked nearby, but it's too far to run with a sharpshooter on us."

Tyler dropped the bloodied tissues to the floor and placed some clean ones on Blade's bleeding arm. "I'll sneak out and find the sniper. If I go out back, Joanna can provide cover fire."

"Can't we switch roles?" she asked, knowing the likely response. But she had to try at least. Her life may already be ebbing away with an advancing tumor. It made sense for her to take this huge risk instead of a strong, healthy person. Why did Tyler not see the logic of this?

Tyler's reply was as she had expected. "No, we can't switch roles." He checked the bullets in the chambers of his gun. Then he cocked his head to the side. "Do I hear sirens?"

The gunfire suddenly ceased, and they all listened carefully for a few seconds.

"Yes," Joanna said. "Luke told us that the police were on their way." She didn't know whether this was now good or bad news. "What do we do now? Make a run for it against the sniper or stay here and get arrested?"

"We take our chances and try to reach Blade's truck," Tyler replied. "We'll leave the motorcycle behind and all go together. Take only what you can easily carry." He grabbed the bag containing the computer equipment, but Blade yanked it back.

"I got this," he said, gripping it tightly. "You take the motorcycle and escape on the woodland paths. The police cars won't be able to follow. We'll meet up afterward."

"No," Tyler said. "No man gets left behind."

The sirens became louder. From the sounds, Joanna guessed that there might be as many as five cars racing their way. But the air was still free of bullets. Maybe the gang's shooters had been scared off.

"There's no warrant out for my arrest," Blade said. "I might be able to talk myself out of a charge even if they do manage to catch me. I can lead them away from you." He pointed to the back door. "We need to get out of here."

"Okay," Tyler said, crawling toward the back door. "I'll take the motorcycle. If the shooting starts up again, return fire and look out for each other." He reached the door and turned the handle. "We'll meet up once we're out of danger."

Tyler slinked out onto the deck and waited for Blade and Joanna to follow.

"Tyler," Joanna yelled in surprise, pointing to Blade's truck, parked about thirty yards away. "Look out."

Behind the truck, partially hidden from view, was a man with a gun, and the barrel was aimed in their direction. A bullet hit the deck and the three friends scrambled to the steps, throwing themselves to the grass where they were afforded a little protection by the large fence post. Joanna knew that if they returned fire, they might damage Blade's only means of transport out of there. If she and Tyler were to escape on the motorcycle, they would leave him trapped. And Tyler had just said that no man got left behind.

Just as the flashing lights of the police cars came into view, a man jumped out from the trees that surrounded the cabin and ran toward them.

He looked to be in his midthirties, wearing combat pants and a black jersey, over which he wore a bulletproof vest. And he held a gun close to his side.

Tyler raised his weapon to shoot, but Joanna held her hand over the barrel.

"No, stop," she said, narrowing her eyes to read the yellow logo on the vest that the man wore. She could just make out the letters FBI. "He's a federal agent."

The man raised his gun, took aim and shot. In the next moment, the guy shielded behind Blade's truck came staggering out, holding his belly. He'd been hit. The next shot from the man's weapon took him down completely. He was dead.

The mystery man lowered his gun. "My name is Hank Carlton," he said, reaching into his pocket and pulling out a badge. "I'm Agent Liam Dennison's handler for the FBI. I just shot and killed a Scorpions sniper in the woods. You need to get out of here before the police arrive. There's a nearby safe house just outside Memphis, at 175 Florence Avenue in Germantown. Meet me there." He glanced behind him. "Go."

"What are you doing here?" Joanna asked. "How did you know about the attack?"

"I didn't," Hank replied. "I heard on the scanner that the police found your hideout, and I wanted to get here before them. I'll stay here and deal with their questions. I'll tell them you escaped. Please trust me. I'm on your side."

"We have no choice but to trust you," Tyler called, as he ran to the garage to fling open the doors. "You're all we've got right now." He looked over at Blade. "Get going, and we'll see you in Memphis."

Tyler's motorcycle roared to life and he steered to Joanna's side, sliding a helmet over her head. Blade was already climbing into his truck, starting up the engine and backing out onto the narrow road that twisted through the park. Joanna hoped he would be able to bypass the police by heading onto one of the many forked roads through the grounds, taking him to the highway and toward Memphis unimpeded.

"Go," repeated Hank, shooing them away.

In a second, Blade was gone and Joanna was jumping onto the back of Tyler's motorcycle, curling her arms around his taut belly.

Tyler revved the engine hard and took the motorcycle into the trees. As he curled his way through the large trunks, Joanna glanced in the rearview mirror to see four police cars screech to a halt outside the cabin. Officers jumped from the vehicles and ran into the woods to pursue, but there was no way they would be able catch Tyler's motorcycle on foot. They gave up their chase quickly, and she watched them stand motionless, navy silhouettes perfectly etched against the snowy sky.

Joanna tried to suppress the excitement surging through her. The exhilaration of their escape was heady, reminding her that she wasn't dead yet, reminding her to live a little while she still could. But at least she hadn't allowed her reckless streak to place others in danger. Tyler's warning had forced her to consider her choices a little more carefully.

Maybe she had conquered this bad habit after all. Or, at least, that's what she chose to think.

One seventy-five Florence Avenue was a well-maintained, large house on a lonely, leafy stretch of road. Germantown was an affluent suburb, with each home possessing a lot of yard space, many with high gates and fences. Even so, Tyler wasn't comfortable in this community. He didn't know the area, people or escape routes. Blade had failed to show up, and the clock was approaching 3:00 p.m. Tyler and Joanna had gotten there first, hidden the motorcycle and awaited the arrival of Hank Carlton, keeping warm by pacing the yard. The FBI agent had turned up just ten minutes ago, saying nothing until he had unlocked the house and ushered them inside, where he was now in the process of checking the place over thoroughly.

Joanna sat impatiently, wide-eyed and alert. The sudden burst of heart-pounding moments seemed to have woken her up. She had a look in her eyes that Tyler recognized. She was hyped up, ready to take on the world. Her instinct to jump to action was clear to see. She believed that her days might be numbered, and she wanted to make them count. He couldn't blame her for that. But it still concerned him nonetheless. He had hoped she would retain her newfound sense of calm. Not just because it was better for their safety, but because it made her more open and honest with him. He tried to not enjoy her company too much, yet he couldn't help himself. Their deep and meaningful conversations were as addictive as any narcotic. When Joanna was calm, he and she were perfect for each other. But when she rushed headlong into danger, they were polar opposites.

"Okay," Hank said, walking down the stairs. "We're all clear." He looked around. "Is it just you two? Where's your friend?"

"I don't know," Tyler said. "Did you see him get away okay?"

"I'm pretty sure he did," Hank replied. "One of the police vehicles pursued him out of the park, but they lost him. He should be careful because they got a partial read on his plate. They know he's from North Carolina, but that's about all they have on him for now."

"I've tried his cell a few times," Tyler said. "But it cuts to voicemail."

Hank sat on the large sofa in the sparsely furnished living room. He was wearing jeans and a white shirt, with his agent's badge around his neck on a cord. His thinning hair, pale skin and bulging middle gave him an appearance of a schoolteacher rather than an agent for the FBI.

"I'm sure he'll get here soon enough," Hank said. "In the meantime, let's talk. Take a seat."

The house was devoid of any homey touches. There were no photographs on the tables, no cushions on the sofas and even the overhead bulb didn't have a shade. The house was also bitterly cold, clearly having had no heat for a long time. The effect was unwelcoming. It simply added to Tyler's discomfort.

"I'd prefer to stand," he said, pulling a scarf from around his neck and placing it around Joanna's. She gave a startled jump but quickly recovered and wound the fabric around her neck, tucking her chin inside.

"As you wish," Hank said, watching Joanna sit on the sofa opposite, rubbing her hands together. She looked to be coiled like a spring, ready to jump to action, but she was doing a decent enough job of keeping it under control.

As he cast his gaze around the entire room, Tyler said, "You said you heard on your scanner that the police were heading our way. Do you know how they found us?"

"They got a positive ID on you from a guy who'd been jogging in the park. He says you jumped him late at night, thinking he was a prowler."

Tyler silently chastised himself. That was a costly mistake.

"Why exactly did you help us escape?" he asked. "You're putting your job on the line."

The FBI agent took a deep breath. "I'll start from the beginning. Agent Liam Dennison has gone missing, and I'm deeply concerned about his well-being. He contacted me last night to request an immediate termination of his undercover assignment. He suspected that The Scorpions had discovered his true identity. I told him to meet me at our arranged rendezvous point at 10:00 p.m., but he never showed. And now he's dropped off the radar." Hank rubbed his hands together anxiously. "Liam is one of the best agents we have out in the field. He'd never go underground without finding a way to contact his handler."

"Is that why you wanted to keep us out of custody?" Tyler asked. "Do you think we might have some information about his location?"

Hank looked Tyler squarely in the eye. "I know

you met with him yesterday at the old prison. You are one of the last people to see him alive—"

"Whoa," Tyler interrupted, holding his hands up in the air. "You said that he'd disappeared. We don't know that he's dead."

Hank hung his head. "I'm afraid we have to prepare for the worst. It's highly likely that Agent Dennison has been killed."

Tyler sat next to Joanna. "Let's not jump to conclusions." He knew that Hank was right, but he didn't want to give up hope. "He may be lying low, waiting for the heat to die down."

"I need to try to piece together Liam's last movements," Hank said. "After he left the prison last night, he dropped Tommy off at his home and then took a cell phone call from one of the senior members of The Scorpions, asking him to go to a bar in Jefferson City for an important meeting. He suspected that this meeting was a hit, so he didn't go. Instead, he called me and asked for help. But I can't place his movements from around 9:00 p.m. onward."

"What about Tommy?" Joanna suggested. "He might know."

Hank laughed, a hard-edged sound. "Tommy's been scared out of his mind by The Dentist, and he's not saying much of anything apparently. I don't know him well, but I don't like him. He's an addict, and I advised Dennison not to use him as an informant." He shrugged. "But Agent Dennison thinks he's honest and reliable. Tommy was with you guys last night, is that right?"

"How do you know that?" Tyler asked.

"Chief Crenshaw told me," Hank replied. "Tommy claims he had important business to discuss with you yesterday."

Tyler narrowed his eyes. "What else did Tommy say?"

"Not much. A couple of federal agents interviewed him this afternoon, but he's staying very tight lipped."

Tyler smiled. "Maybe he's not as flaky as he looks."

"How did he find you in Tennessee?" Hank asked. "And, more importantly, why did he make the dangerous visit to come to see you?"

"It was actually Dennison who found us," Tyler replied. "And he sent Tommy with some information regarding The Scorpions investigation."

Hank stood, a look of surprise on his face. "What kind of information?"

Tyler suddenly realized how little he knew about Hank Carlton. How much could they trust Dennison's handler?

"Agent Dennison entrusted us with some vital evidence regarding the possible identity of Mr. X," Tyler said, watching Hank wring his hands in agitation, checking behind the drapes, probably looking out for Blade. "We've already made arrangements to pass this information along to a trustworthy source in the police force."

Hank sat back down. "Can I ask who that might be?"

Tyler smiled. "You can ask, but I'm not gonna tell. As soon as Blade arrives, we'll be leaving."

Hank laughed, but not happily. "I think you guys have some kind of death wish." He gestured to the room around him. "This is a safe, secure and comfortable environment, where you can stay until we get to the truth."

He turned to Joanna. "I believe you when you say you were set up, Deputy Graham, and I want to help you unmask Mr. X. Liam made it clear to me that he trusted you, so I have no interest in arresting you or your sheriff. I can shield you."

"That's very kind of you, Hank," Joanna said. "But Tyler's right. I was all ready to come tearing down here yesterday with Tommy before I'd had the chance to think it through. We should hand over the evidence to somebody we know and trust. We literally just met you. We've got to be cautious."

Hank sighed deeply. "I hope you know what you're doing. According to Crenshaw, Tommy claims that he was followed on his way back from Tennessee. It's totally spooked him and, as soon as he got back to Godspeed, he walked into the police station and requested around the clock protection. He's scared out of his mind." He leaned forward and spoke softly, as if his whispered words would have more impact. "If The Scorpions found Tommy, they could find you. Don't be complacent. Stay here for a while."

"Can I ask you a question, Hank?" Tyler said. "Did Agent Dennison ever mention Chief Crenshaw to you?"

"Yes. He told me that the chief had started making plenty of visits to the old prison, meeting with high profile gang members. Liam was in the process of compiling a dossier of evidence against him." Hank snapped his fingers. "That's what Tommy gave you, isn't it? He gave you evidence that implicates Crenshaw."

Tyler felt safe to admit the truth. "Yes, he did. We have a number of photographs that show Chief Crenshaw at the prison, although they haven't yet been verified as authentic. We need to get them scrutinized by an expert."

Hank turned on a lamp next to him. "May I see them?"

Tyler took the photographs from the bag at his feet, sliding them to Hank across the coffee table. When Hank picked them up, he flicked through them slowly, taking time to study each one. "These look genuine to me." He looked over at Tyler. "This could be enough to build a solid case against Crenshaw. I'll make some calls and get more agents down here. I don't think you guys should be going anywhere. It's Christmas Eve tomorrow." He smiled. "We can even get you a tree and a turkey and turn the heat on. What do you say?"

Tyler felt a sense of unease descend. Hank seemed determined to keep them there in Germantown. Was it truly to safeguard their lives, or was he more interested in ensuring they would be open to another attack?

"It seems a little odd that you just happened to stumble on the men who attacked us today," Tyler said. "Why were you alone? You had no backup at all." He cast his eyes around the room. "And why are you the only agent here? Tommy led us to believe that there would be a team of Feds here. This place feels like it hasn't been heated in weeks."

Hank's face broke into an amused grin. "So now *I'm* under suspicion?"

"I'd just like an explanation," Tyler replied. "I'm not accusing you of anything."

"Like I already told you, I went to your cabin this morning to warn you about the imminent arrival of the Tennessee police," Hank said. "When I heard your location on the scanner, I had no time to summon another agent. I'd hoped that

Agent Dennison would be with you or you'd know where he is." He laced his fingers together and pulled them taut around his nape. "But when I arrived, I saw that The Scorpions had beaten me to it. Two gunmen were firing on you, and I did what I could to help." He raised an eyebrow. "But you don't have to thank me."

Tyler looked down at the floor, slightly shame-faced. In all the drama, he hadn't thanked the man who had helped them escape both death and arrest.

"We really appreciate what you've done for us, Hank," he said. "But like Joanna said, we literally only just met you. And I'm not comfortable here. This could be a trap. Where are the other agents that Tommy talked about?"

"They're out on assignments, but a couple of them will be here soon," Hank replied tersely, seeming to take offense. "Federal agents are busy people, Sheriff. They don't have time to sit around twenty-four hours a day."

Tyler stood and looked out the window. Where was Blade? Time was ticking by, and he didn't want to be there any longer. Something didn't feel right. "I'd like to leave," he said, picking up the photographs from a side table. "I have an important appointment to keep."

Hank tried to repair their strained conversation. "I'm sorry. I guess I should've expected this level of caution from a former SEAL." He reached into his pocket and took out a white card, placing it on the table. "Here's my contact number. If you insist on leaving, I hope you'll call me if you run into any trouble." He watched Tyler pick it up and place it in his pocket. "How's the memory now? I heard you suffered a bad blow to the head at the prison."

Tyler rubbed his palms together. The skin was dry and cracked. "I'm recovering well," he said, unwilling to reveal too much. His stomach growled, reminding him of the need to eat.

"You sound hungry," Hank said. "I can get you something to eat before you leave." He checked his watch, as if anxious for the other agents to arrive. "What would you like?"

Tyler looked at Joanna. She had surprised him by saying very little during his conversation with Hank, but on locking eyes with her, he saw the reason why. She was miles away, her eyes focused on a point on the floor.

"Joanna," he said. "Would you like to eat?"

Her eyes snapped up to his. "No, I'd like to get going. We can get some food on the way."

He gave her a big smile. At least they were on the same page. But his smile quickly faded. "We can't leave without Blade," he said. "No way."

Then, as if Tyler's prayer was answered, a soft knock sounded at the window, and Blade's face peered in through the glass, his cheeks framed with cupped hands. His breath created a patch of steam on the pane, and he appeared to be cold, tired and dirty. But he was safe.

"At last," Hank said, rising. "I'll let him in."

Tyler grabbed his bag from the floor. "No need, Hank. We're leaving."

Joanna and Tyler sat in the back of Blade's truck as they headed out of the Memphis area in the direction of the Missouri border. Blade's hands were caked in grime, and his cheeks were streaked with black marks, which he rubbed at with a cloth. While traveling to the safe house, the truck had broken down, forcing Blade to undertake repairs at the side of the road.

"It's a good thing I'm a mechanic, huh?" he said, looking at them both through the rearview mirror. "Somebody had tampered with the engine, obviously trying to isolate us on the roadside if we managed to get away." He tapped the steering wheel with his fingers. "But she's been put back into good shape."

Joanna fidgeted with her necklace. "Do you think it was wise to leave the motorcycle behind? It's so much faster than this truck."

"We're fortunate that we managed to get to the safe house without being pulled over by the cops," Tyler said. "A description of that motorcycle has probably been distributed to every county in Tennessee. This truck may be slower, but it's safer."

"But the police will be looking for a truck with a North Carolina plate," Joanna said. "We should've taken Hank up on his offer of a borrowed car."

Tyler had already firmly declined the offer when it was made. "I'd rather take my chances in the truck. Hank was far too pushy for my liking." He took the agent's card from his pocket. "I'll only contact him if I really have no choice."

"I agree," Blade said. "It was like he was stalling us when we tried to leave. And he kept checking his watch. He seemed on edge."

Joanna had more sympathy for Hank than Tyler and Blade did. "Of course he was on edge. His field agent has probably just been murdered, and he wants to stop any more deaths."

"Perhaps," Tyler said. "But we should stick to the plan we made. If Luke is as reliable as you say, then he'll be persistent in getting the photographs of Crenshaw to the right people." His stomach growled again. "But before we do anything, we should stop for food. Blade, pull over at the next gas station or drive-through, would you?"

Irritated, Joanna let out a long breath. This was

yet another delay. Tyler put a hand on top of hers. "We have plenty of time."

Joanna forced a smile. "I'm trying really hard to be patient, but I just want to get the ball rolling on arresting Crenshaw." She looked out the window and breathed deeply to bring her heart rate down. "It's the breakthrough that we needed. We could return to Godspeed as heroes instead of felons."

Tyler shifted a little closer to her and brought his mouth to her ear. "Patience is better than pride. We don't want to be heroes. We just want to expose the truth."

Joanna felt sufficiently humbled. "Patience isn't something that I'm overly blessed with. I've taken to heart what you said to me about keeping a lid on my impulsive tendencies. But it's not an easy thing to switch off."

"I know," he said, slipping an arm around her shoulders. She winced as his hand brushed against her tender swelling, and he repositioned his fingers, splaying them wide on her shoulder.

"Whatever else happens today," he said, "I'm taking you to see Dr. Sinclair at Godspeed General Hospital. I called him this morning, and he's prepared to see you in secret this evening. We'll go see him right after I meet with Luke."

Joanna rested her head on Tyler's shoulder, knowing that seeing a doctor was the most sensible thing she could do. "I'm not going to argue this time. I need to know one way or the other."

She felt Tyler rest his chin on her head. "I'm glad."

"You were right about me being scared," she said. "I know it's fear that makes me act recklessly sometimes, and I'm grateful you've helped me come to that realization." She lifted her head. "Even so, I might need you to remind me every now and again."

"Of course," he said. "I want to help you, Joanna, but it's been difficult for me to know what to say. You're obviously an excellent deputy in so many ways, and I didn't want to make you feel inadequate"

"But you still have to pull me in line," she said. "I get that now."

Joanna thought of all the times Sheriff Beck had tried to discipline her in the past, and how she had pushed back against him, causing her to almost be suspended on one occasion. But his memory loss seemed to have changed everything. With no recollection of their past, Tyler had been able to start afresh with her, not allowing his pre-existing knowledge to cloud his judgment. But now that his memory was returning, how long would it take until he remembered their petty squabbles? How long would it take until he recalled the moment she called him a coward for refusing to allow her to rush inside a burning house to rescue its occupants? Moments later, the building collapsed and the firefighters arrived to search through the debris for survivors with specialist equipment. Tyler had saved her from certain death, but she had been ungracious and indifferent. And now she felt ashamed by it.

She gazed at him, wondering what was going through his mind. His face was so close to hers that she could see the faint lines around his eyes and mouth. She had never noticed them before. Were they the result of the stress of the assignment he had undertaken for her benefit?

"What about you?" she asked. "Are any more memories coming back?"

"Yeah," he answered. "Quite a lot actually."

Blade's voice broke through their conversation. "I'll stop here at this diner and get us something to go. It's safer if you stay out of sight." He pointed to a large tree, its branches heavy and curved under the weight of snow. "I'll park here, where it's nice and quiet." He pulled into the lot and slowly came to a halt. "I'll get some sandwiches or something. I'll also take a look at the injury on my arm in the bathroom so don't worry if I'm gone a few minutes."

"We're not going anywhere," Tyler said. "Thanks, Blade."

Blade raised his eyebrows as he opened the

truck door. "I figured you could do with a few minutes alone anyway."

Joanna watched him walk from the truck, his distinctive gait trudging through the freshly fallen snow to reach the cleared path to the diner. The eatery was a tiny, quaint old railway carriage festooned with Christmas lights, candy canes, plastic reindeer and even a life-size dancing Santa. The overt display of festive cheer made her feel empty inside. Would she really be facing the holiday season as a fugitive? And what's more, would she be spending it with a man who was just beginning to recover his memories of her insubordination?

"So," she said tentatively. "What kind of things do you remember?" She hooked her hair behind her ears awkwardly. "Anything about me?"

Tyler's gaze left hers and traveled to the brightly lit diner. "No," he said. "I still don't recall much about my life as a sheriff, but I'm starting to remember my home and my neighborhood. I guess that the memories of you must be reluctant to reveal themselves." He turned and smiled. "Any idea why?"

Joanna shook her head, feeling a mixture of relief tinged with disappointment. She had been worried that Tyler would remember their troubled history, yet she was saddened by the fact that his brain continued to block her out of his past. Was his subconscious trying to erase her?

He must have noticed the disappointment on her face. "I don't think that memories are coming back in order of importance," he said. "It's just random." He put an index finger to his head. "You're in here for sure."

She smiled self-consciously. Tyler had read her like a book. He had seen her desire to be important to him, and she was embarrassed. She was his deputy and nothing more. She didn't deserve center stage in his head, and she would have to accept relegation to the sidelines of his fragile memory. At least this would mean they could return to Godspeed and pick up where they left off: as bickering colleagues who disagreed on almost everything. She should be pleased.

So why did it hurt quite so much?

As Blade continued their journey into Missouri, Tyler dug into his hot roast beef sandwich, despite the fact that his appetite had dwindled away to nothing. All he could focus on was Joanna's presence by his side. He had just lied to her, something he had promised they would never do with each other. When she had asked if his memories of her were returning, he found it easier to say no. In truth, he *did* remember his relationship with her, or at least some of it. He recalled snatches of heated conversations, her rebelliousness, her occasional refusal to carry out a direct order. His old frustrations and irritations had been brought to the fore, and no matter how hard he tried to push them down, it altered the way he now saw Joanna.

Yet he had grown incredibly close to her recently, and she had shared her deepest fears with him. It was as though she were two people. The Joanna he had gotten to know over the last three days wasn't the same deputy he was now remembering. She was calmer, more restrained and learning to harness her fears. And he had been allowing himself to fall in love with her.

He stopped eating as this thought hit him in the gut. He stole a glance at Joanna. Their closeness had crept a little further forward with each conversation, and he admired her resilience and courage in dealing with her cancer fears. He liked the way she was open about her struggles with her faith, not hiding her anger with God. She was brave and honest and belligerent and more complicated than he could ever possibly imagine. It would be hard for most men to love her, but not for Tyler. For him it would be as easy as falling from a log.

But the question that burned on his mind was: could he take the risk? He had dated her once and gotten burned. No matter how much his heart wanted him to hold Joanna in his arms, his head told him to back off. And Tyler, always the methodical and meticulous sheriff, obeyed his head over his heart at all times.

NINE

Tyler handed his cell phone to Blade and led him a few steps away from the truck, which had been well hidden on an old dirt road close to the former prison.

"Take this," Tyler said, pressing the cell into Blade's hand. "If anything happens to me, please call Dr. Sinclair from Godspeed General Hospital. I've already spoken to him about Joanna's health situation." He glanced over Blade's shoulder to see Joanna engrossed in the task of adjusting a pair of binoculars. "He's agreed to carry out some tests free of charge."

Blade's face showed its concern. "What's wrong with Joanna? She looks fine to me."

"You need to know that she's a cancer survivor," Tyler said. "And she's been having some pain. She wants to see a medical professional to rule out a return of a tumor."

Blade ran a hand down his face. "Oh man, that sucks." He slipped Tyler's cell into his pocket.

"Of course you can rely on me to help her." He put a hand on his friend's shoulder. "I'm sorry, Tyler. I know you're close to Joanna. This must be hard for you."

"Not as hard for me as it is for her," he said. "But we'll face whatever comes our way." He stepped a little closer to Blade. "I know you had some apprehensions about trusting her…"

Blade stepped back and cut Tyler off with a wave of his hand. "I have zero worries about her now. You said that your gut, your head and your heart told you to trust her. And you were right." He smiled. "I should've learned by now that you're always right. She's one of us through and through." He dropped his voice to barely a whisper. "And she seems to have gotten a handle on her gung-ho attitude, as well. Whatever you said to her seems to have worked."

"I can't take all the credit for that," Tyler said. "The hard work is all her own." He checked his watch. "I should get going."

Blade held out the fingerprints he had processed from the glass. "You want to take these? It would save us the trouble of breaking into the sheriff's department to access the FBI database."

Tyler thought long and hard before answering. "No, let's not put all our eggs in one basket, just in case something bad happens. If Luke proves trustworthy, we can send him these prints electronically. But I'd rather be cautious right now."

He then walked over to the truck and took out a box of ammunition, dropping it into a backpack and zipping it. Joanna scanned the area with binoculars, a look of pure concentration on her face.

"I see nothing," she said, lowering the binoculars. "I hope Luke turns up. We'll be watching."

"Remember," he said, slipping his arms through the backpack, where the photographs of Crenshaw were safely tucked away. "Don't reveal yourselves, whatever happens to me. Okay?"

"Stay safe, Tyler." Joanna held out her hand awkwardly. He realized that she was offering it to shake, but he pulled her into an embrace. She was taken aback at first but relaxed into his arms, breathing heavily on his neck.

"Promise me that you'll keep away from the prison," he said, drawing back and locking eyes with her. "I mean it. No matter what, you and Blade must not try to come to my rescue."

She nodded. "Agreed."

A couple of days ago, he'd never have believed these words, but now he did. Joanna was slowly becoming the steady and dependable deputy he always knew she could be. She often took two steps forward and one step back, but her progress was consistent. And his affection for her grew a little bit more each hour that passed.

Blade slapped him on the back. "Nothing bad is gonna happen, Tyler," he said. "You'll hand the photographs to Luke and walk calmly back to the truck. We'll see you in no time."

Tyler shook Blade's hand and walked from the cover of trees, heading out on the wide open wasteland that surrounded the prison. The huge structure dominated the skyline from this focal point, its towers jutting into the white, luminous sky like a medieval fortress. The snow whipping its way across the land made the vista appear like some vast, dystopian film set. No life seemed to thrive in this landscape, and the graffiti painted on the crumbling walls gave clues about its delinquent visitors. Tyler turned up the collar on his coat and vowed to lobby the state legislature to demolish the building as soon as he could.

As he approached the front entrance with its high rusted gates and broken fence, he saw a police car in the distance heading his way, creating new tire tracks on the brilliant white ground. He continued his path and stopped right in front of the old guard's hut, now corroded and stained by weather. The vehicle came closer, and Tyler could clearly see that it was a sheriff's cruiser with a lone man sitting in the driver's seat. He knew that this man was Luke. The rounded face and jowly neck were recognizable to him, filling him with a sense of reassurance and safety.

Tyler waited for the car to grind to a slow, crunching halt in front of him and waved a greeting. Yet when Luke exited the car, he immediately knew that something was wrong. The deputy's face was pained and tense.

"I'm sorry, Sheriff," Luke said, as Tyler noticed the back doors of the cruiser opening. "Chief Crenshaw discovered our emails and I had no choice but to bring him here. He threatened to arrest me if I didn't cooperate."

Tyler looked skyward and let out an almighty groan as Chief George Crenshaw came into view, closely followed by Mayor Harley Landon. They had hidden themselves in the backseat, crouching low and remaining unseen until the last moment.

"Howdy, Sheriff," Chief Crenshaw said, placing his hat firmly on his head. "Must be a surprise to see me, ain't it?"

Tyler saw no point in running. "I'm guessing you're here to arrest me," he said, flicking his eyes over to Mayor Landon. "And I see you've brought your favorite sidekick along with you."

Mayor Landon was clearly unhappy at Tyler's tone of voice. "Chief Crenshaw's been overworked since you decided to go AWOL, what with all the press conferences and media interviews." Landon looked over at the chief. "So I'm assisting him in carrying out some of his extra duties."

Tyler couldn't stop himself from laughing out loud. "You're just here for the entertainment, right, Mayor?"

Landon pursed his lips, and his nostrils flared. "Like I said, George is a very busy man these days, what with running his own station as well as worrying about yours. And on top of that, he heads up the drug task force."

As if emphasizing the point, Crenshaw dug into his pants pockets and pulled out a large set of keys. "I now have access to almost every public building in Godspeed," he said proudly. "I practically run this town."

Tyler didn't like this overt display of power. "You got keys for the sheriff's department there, too?" he asked. "Because you have no right to meddle in my station's business."

"I only have a key for safe keeping," Crenshaw said with a smug smile. "With only one deputy running the place, I thought it wise to get a copy made for myself from Luke's set." He shook his head. "The sheriff's office has been so poorly managed recently, I figured I should take a peek inside every now and again."

"You're power crazed," Tyler called angrily. "I'm the elected sheriff, not you."

Crenshaw was impassive. "I'm guessing that your days as sheriff are over, Tyler."

"Don't count on it, George. I'll be back."

Crenshaw started walking toward Tyler, keeping his hand resting on his holstered weapon. His jaw moved rhythmically as he slowly chewed gum. "First you have to face justice in the courts for evading arrest. I don't want to have to pull out my gun or cuff you. You're a sheriff, and I'd like to show you some respect. So can you please hand over the evidence that you were discussing with Deputy Hutchence, and I'll take you to Godspeed station for questioning."

Tyler didn't move. A list of possibilities ran through his mind. Once Crenshaw had the photographs, he could destroy them immediately.

"Come on, Tyler," the chief said. "Let's not fight anymore. Police officers are dying at the hands of drug dealers, and we have to stop them. I want to expose the ringleader of The Scorpions as much as you do."

Tyler didn't believe this for a second. And he knew he had to protect the photographs at all costs. He wondered if he might be able to surreptitiously hand them over to Luke when Crenshaw was distracted.

"Just arrest me already," he said, holding his wrists in midair. "I won't put up a fight."

Chief Crenshaw jerked his head to Tyler. "Luke," he said. "Get the bag and check what's inside."

Tyler held his breath as Luke walked over,

slid the backpack from Tyler's shoulder and unzipped it.

"Take the photographs," Tyler whispered, bowing his head to avoid his lips being seen. "Hide them."

But Landon was watching his every move. "What did you say, Sheriff?" he asked loudly, coming to stand next to Luke. "What was that about photographs?" He grabbed the bag from Luke and turned it upside down, scattering the pictures on the snowy ground. Tyler watched in dismay as moisture seeped through the paper, destroying the clarity of the images.

"What on Earth is this?" Chief Crenshaw shouted, staring at the photos littering the ground. "Where did you get these?"

Tyler said nothing.

The chief bent to retrieve some of the pictures, shaking his head in apparent disbelief. "These are all faked," he shouted, snatching up the rest. "Somebody's trying to frame me." He crumpled the photographs in his fists, turning his fury on Tyler. "*You* are trying to frame me, trying to get me suspended so you can take the heat off your corrupt deputy." He raised one hand to the sky in a dramatic gesture. "I don't think I know who you are anymore, Sheriff."

Tyler knew better than to anger the chief any further by raising his voice to the same level. He spoke quietly and slowly. "These photographs came from Liam Dennison, an FBI agent who was working undercover in The Scorpions until his sudden disappearance yesterday. They were delivered to me by his informant, Tommy Roper."

"What?" the chief yelled. "You mean that skinny little meth head who wants around the clock police protection? He's a waste of space. The Feds took him away this afternoon, and I'm glad to be rid of him. I'm always on his case for hanging around drug dealers on the streets. He hates me. He probably Photoshopped these on his computer just to cause me trouble."

Tyler narrowed his eyes at the chief. Crenshaw looked and sounded genuinely shocked to discover his face in these photographs. Could they really be faked? But then he thought of the other clues pointing toward the chief being Mr. X: the cigar butts on the ground and the lack of care he had taken to follow procedure when setting up the undercover investigation.

Crenshaw held the crumpled photographs under Tyler's nose. "I expect you were hoping to get me arrested with this forged evidence, huh? I suppose you're also behind all the funny business down at the station."

"What are you talking about, George?"

"Things keep getting moved around, and paperwork relating to The Scorpions case is going missing." Crenshaw spit his chewing gum onto the ground. "I reckon that somebody is getting in the station at night, trying to find and destroy evidence."

"And you think I'd be stupid enough to break in to Godspeed police station?" Tyler asked, uncertain if the chief was spinning him a yarn, trying to pull him off track.

Crenshaw snorted. "I think you'd do anything to get your pretty little girlfriend off the hook."

Tyler didn't like what he was hearing. The chief obviously didn't like Joanna, and his vendetta was personal. "These photographs need to be logged as evidence and analyzed by an expert," he said. "If they're forged, then you have nothing to worry about."

He then turned his head to Luke. "Deputy Hutchence should take charge of this, as it involves a serious conflict of interest on your part." Tyler looked at the mass of crumpled photographic paper in the chief's arms. "So please stop damaging those pictures any further, and do your job. Either arrest me or let me go."

At this, Mayor Landon seemed to spring to life. "Are you gonna let him talk to you like that, George?" He pointed a finger at Tyler's chest, stopping just short of making contact. "Your name may be Beck, but that doesn't mean the chief is at your beck and call." He stood back and folded his arms, satisfied with his clever play on words. "You're not our sheriff anymore. You were officially suspended three days ago."

Harley's irate tirade had a galvanizing effect on Chief Crenshaw. "Deputy Hutchence," he said, handing the photographs to Luke. "Take these to the cruiser, smooth them out and find a plastic wallet for them."

Then he turned to Tyler, roughly pulled his arms around his back and secured a pair of cuffs on his wrists. "Tyler Beck," he said, clearly attempting to inject some gravitas into his voice, "I am arresting you for harboring a fugitive and evading arrest."

Mayor Landon laughed scornfully as he headed back to the car, clearly enjoying his moment of authority over the popular Yardley sheriff.

"Once Sheriff Beck is in a cell, I'm sure that Deputy Graham won't be far behind," the mayor said. "She never could stay out of danger. She's a real firecracker, that one."

"Actually," Tyler said, allowing the chief to lead him by the elbow to the car. "I wouldn't hold your breath waiting for Deputy Graham to show up. She's got much more important things to do."

"Well, we'll just have to see about that, won't we," Crenshaw said mockingly. "Because if I know Joanna Graham, she won't be able to resist coming to rescue you. Time will tell."

Tyler sat in the back of the car while Luke secured his belt.

"Sorry, sir," Luke muttered. "I never meant for any of this to happen. I hope Joanna is safe and well."

Tyler didn't answer. Instead he said a silent prayer. He was pretty hopeful that Chief Crenshaw was wrong about Joanna rushing to rescue him, but the chief was definitely right about one thing: only time would tell.

Joanna sat in the brightly lit white room, absentmindedly reading a chart on the wall explaining the causes of hypertension. She had hoped it would help take her mind off Tyler while she waited for Dr. Sinclair to get her samples checked, but the minutes ticked by tortuously. The doctor had been incredibly kind in seeing her immediately, and had taken great care to smuggle her into his hospital consulting room from the parking lot. Joanna had known Wayne Sinclair since they were children, and they had attended the same Sunday school every week. Their friendship had faded over the years, but Dr. Sinclair clearly knew Joanna's character and saw through the trumped-up charges. After examining her swelling, his face had been grave and he had drawn a blood sample to analyze for tumor markers. Now he was rushing that sample through the system so she could have an immediate result.

She sighed heavily and put her head in her hands, her mind replaying the scene at the prison. She and Blade had watched helplessly as Tyler was arrested and placed in Luke's cruiser by Chief Crenshaw.

"Hey, Joanna," Blade said, leaning against the wall by the door. "Worrying isn't going to help. I know it's hard, but try to relax."

She looked over at him. Right at that moment, she wished with all her heart that he were Tyler. She imagined the sheriff standing in front of her, in full uniform, a hand resting on his holster and his hat positioned with the brim low, as he always liked to wear it, so that his eyes appeared dark and brooding in the shadow.

"I should be helping Tyler instead of sitting here, twiddling my thumbs," she said. "I can't let him sit in a jail cell."

"What exactly do you think you can do to help him?" Blade asked, sitting down on a chair next to her. "You'd just end up being arrested along with him. I told Tyler that I'd take you to see Dr. Sinclair if anything happened to him, and I kept that promise. I've left a message for Hank to call me back right away."

"Hank?" she questioned. "I thought Tyler didn't fully trust him yet."

"Hank's the only person who can bail Tyler out quickly," Blade said. "We don't have a choice. We gotta trust him."

Joanna raised her eyes to the ceiling. The whiteness of the room hurt her eyes, and she felt cold, shivery even. Was this a symptom of her cancer?

Blade put an arm around her shoulders. It was an awkward gesture, and he was clearly uncomfortable with the physical contact, but she appreciated his sentiment.

"I know you wish Tyler was here with you now instead of me," he said. "But I'll do all I can to keep you out of trouble until the two of you are reunited."

She smiled as her color rose. Was it really so obvious where her affections lay?

Blade smiled back at her. "However much you're missing Tyler, I guarantee that he's missing you twice as much, but he would never want you to place yourself at risk for him." His cell phone began to ring, and he jumped from his seat to open the door, almost colliding with Dr. Sinclair as the young physician entered the room. "It's Hank," Blade said, glancing back at Joanna. "I'll take it in the hallway while you and the doctor talk."

He disappeared through the door, and Dr. Sinclair closed it firmly behind him before taking his seat at the desk in the room. He moved slowly, taking his time, and Joanna began to wonder if the doctor was figuring out how to break the test results to her.

"Just give it to me straight, Doc," she said with an awkward laugh, desperately trying to lighten the somber atmosphere.

Dr. Sinclair didn't smile or laugh in response. He simply put his forearms on the desk, clasped his hands together and leaned forward, regarding her with an expression of sympathy.

She dropped her lighthearted approach. "It's bad news, isn't it?"

"Before I give you the results of your blood test," the doctor said, "it's important to explain that the presence of tumor markers is not a definite diagnosis of cancer. Without a biopsy, we can't know for sure that your cancer had returned."

Joanna knew where this conversation was leading. "But the presence of tumor markers makes it highly likely that a tumor is growing, right?"

"Yes."

She took a deep breath. "And my blood sample has tumor markers, doesn't it?"

The doctor took his time in answering. "Joanna, I wish you'd reconsider your decision to remain on the run from the authorities. I'd desperately like to run a biopsy on the lump in your armpit. It's the only way to be sure. But I can't do the biopsy without inputting your insurance details into the patient database."

"Wayne," Joanna said, raising her voice. "We've known each other too long to pretend that you can change my mind. I'm really grateful that you took a risk in seeing me on such short notice, and I promise I'll never tell a single person what you've done for me tonight. Once I've managed to clear my name, I'll come back and get the biopsy done, and I'll agree to whatever schedule of treatment you think I need, but until that time, I'd appreciate you giving me the results of my blood test."

The doctor leaned back in his chair. "Your bloodwork showed an abnormal level of tumor markers that are indicative of the presence of breast cancer."

"So it's back?"

The doctor nodded slowly. "It seems likely, although I can't give a firm diagnosis without further investigation."

"Is the cancer the cause of the pain I have?" she asked.

"No. You also have a large bruise in that area. Did you injure yourself somehow?"

"Yes, I fell against a wall recently." She reached around and gently touched the swelling. "I've been telling myself that the bruise was the reason for the pain."

"Actually," the doctor said, "the bruise *is* the cause of the pain and most of the swelling. It's a blessing that you received this injury because without it you probably wouldn't have noticed the lump underneath for another few months. It looks like we've caught this early. You're fortunate in that sense."

Fortunate or *blessed* wouldn't be the words Joanna would have chosen right at that moment. She stood briskly and pulled on her jacket. "Thank you, Doctor, you've been really helpful."

Dr. Sinclair rose with her. "Do you have to leave right now? I thought we could discuss this in more detail." He put a hand on her shoulder. "It's almost Christmas, Joanna. I don't want you to be worrying about your health over the holidays. Can't you at least tell me how to reach you?"

"No," she said quickly. "If I have any concerns, I can call."

"It's important that you look after yourself. You mentioned that you've been feeling tired lately. Do you have anybody to take care of you if you feel unwell?"

Joanna closed her eyes, a sudden pain building in her chest. "I'm hoping that the footprints in the sand are taking care of me."

She opened her eyes to see a flash of confusion fall over Dr. Sinclair's face, so she quickly added, "I'll be with Sheriff Beck. I'm in safe hands with him."

The doctor raised his eyebrows, obviously remembering how Tyler had previously left the hospital without being formally discharged. "How's the sheriff doing? I've been deeply worried about him. Any memories recovered yet?"

"He's doing okay," Joanna replied, inching her way toward the door, anxious to leave and check on his status. "He's remembering more and more each day."

"This is good news," Dr. Sinclair said. "I'd like to see both of you back here for an assessment in a week's time. Do you think you could manage that?"

"Um…I'm not sure." She rested her hand on the door handle. "I really have to go now. Should I leave the hospital the same way we came in?"

"Yes, it's the pharmaceuticals delivery route, so nobody will be using it at this time of night. But please take care of yourself wherever you go. And call my office if you're worried or you need to see me."

"Thank you, Wayne."

She opened the door and saw Blade in the hall-way, slipping his cellphone into his pocket.

"You okay, Joanna?" he asked. "You look pale."

"Yeah," she said, grabbing his coat sleeve and leading him away from the doctor's office. "It's not important. We've got more pressing matters to attend to."

She strode into the dark, quiet corridor and walked rapidly to the exit. Her heart was pumping with an all too familiar feeling, telling her to rush out and save the world. If her presence on this Earth was certain to be cut short, she needed to make the most of the time she had left. Rather than dying in a hospital bed, weak and frail, she would go out in a blaze of glory. A return to her old, reckless habits would be sure to destroy the intimacy she had built up with Tyler, but what did it matter? They had no real future anyway. It was only a matter of time before Tyler remembered how incompatible they were, only a matter of time before their burgeoning relationship imploded. She'd been a fool to consider that she and Tyler could ever fall in love. It had been a ridiculous fantasy that she now firmly erased from her mind.

Whatever progress she had made so far would be lost, because the old Joanna was back. And this time she was here to stay.

* * *

Chief George Crenshaw reluctantly handed Tyler his weapon, ammunition and other personal effects. After Tyler had been held overnight at the Godspeed police station, Hank had arrived in the early morning with a bail order, signed by a judge, forcing Crenshaw to release his prisoner immediately.

"Just remember, Tyler," Crenshaw said, regarding Hank suspiciously. "Your bail conditions require you to stay within the boundaries of Yardley County at all times. You got that?"

Tyler gave the chief a curt nod while holstering his weapon.

"And if you attempt to meet up with Deputy Graham, I'll rearrest you," Crenshaw continued. "I'll be checking up on you."

"I don't doubt it," Tyler muttered, sliding his bag onto his back and heading toward the exit.

"Oh, I almost forgot," Crenshaw said as Hank opened the door to let in a blast of icy air. "Deputy Hutchence has got an expert looking at those photographs of yours. Early indications say that they're all faked." He smiled, showing his small, neat rows of nicotine-stained teeth. "So it looks like you got duped by that little meth head."

Tyler stopped in his tracks and turned slowly

to look at the chief. He didn't want to give any emotion away. "Early indications can be wrong, Chief."

"They won't be," Crenshaw said curtly. "I'm thankful that the folks at city hall are allowing me to remain in my post while the investigation into these pictures is completed." He crossed his arms. "So your attempt to slander me hasn't paid off."

Tyler saw no point in arguing with the chief any further. He was cold, tired, hungry and desperate to see Joanna. He had missed her more than he would care to admit.

"Merry Christmas," Crenshaw boomed sarcastically as Tyler stepped onto the snowy sidewalk. "Enjoy the holidays."

Tyler looked to the sky. It was Christmas Eve, and he wanted to spend the day in front of a cozy fire, appreciating the cinnamon smells wafting from the kitchen, watching old TV shows, wrapping gifts, preparing his suit for church in the morning, sitting down around a family table. He rubbed at his temples as it occurred to him that the holiday season suddenly held much more meaning than it used to. He'd clearly changed a great deal. He was softer, gentler and more paternal. He wanted his own family around him. When he was a SEAL, he'd always spent Christmas at the base in Virginia. He had some distant relatives living in Texas, but other than that, he had no family to speak of. Maybe this was why he returned to Godspeed. Maybe he had wanted to lay down roots after all. Joanna had already told him as much, but he hadn't felt it in his heart. Not until now.

"I've arranged for you to meet Joanna and Blade at a remote location across the county line and away from prying eyes," Hank said, opening the passenger door for Tyler. "I'm hoping you trust me enough to allow me to take you there."

Tyler sat in the car, his anxiety to see Joanna growing. "To be perfectly honest with you, Hank, I'm at a loss for who to trust. If those photographs of Crenshaw *are* faked, who is responsible? Is it Dennison or Tommy or somebody else? Who's trying to mislead the investigation?"

"I'm afraid I can't ask Agent Dennison that question," replied Hank, sitting in the driver's seat, "because he was found on the banks of the Mississippi this morning with his throat cut."

Tyler put his head in his hands. "No."

"Tommy Roper is currently in FBI protective custody, and the Organized Crime Unit's investigation into The Scorpions has been temporarily suspended. We don't want to lose any more agents." He tapped the wheel with his index finger as he drove. "Agent Dennison didn't deserve to die like that. It's inhuman."

"I'm sorry," Tyler said. "I really am."

He then leaned back in his seat, knowing that his words inadequately expressed his sense of sadness. He looked around, trying to find inspiration, only to lock eyes on a pack of cigars slotted into the pocket of the driver's door. They were the same brand as Chief Crenshaw's. His heart started to thump in his chest.

"I didn't know you were a smoker, Hank," he said, as casually as he could, pointing toward the cigars. "It's not good for you, you know."

"I don't smoke often," Hank said. "A pack lasts me a whole month usually." He glanced at Tyler. "Do you want one, Sheriff?"

"No, thanks."

Hank pulled the pack from the door and held it up. "You don't mind if I…"

Tyler shook his head and concentrated on watching the road ahead, glad that Hank would have a temporary distraction. Tyler didn't want to make further conversation. He wanted to focus hard on trying to remember the eyes of the man who attacked him in the prison. He had been convinced it was Crenshaw, but that assumption had now been challenged. Could Hank have been the culprit leaving butts on the floor at the old prison? If he was a regular visitor there, he could've smoked plenty of cigars while overseeing his operation, dropping the ends and leaving unintended traces of himself behind. Could this federal agent be Mr. X?

The journey to the remote location gave Tyler plenty of time to mull over these thoughts, and he was still nowhere near a conclusion when Hank pulled his car into an old farmstead, dilapidated and uninhabited, gray and creepy behind a blanket of freezing fog rolling from the river. They were somewhere on the Kentucky Bend, where the mighty Mississippi curled in a loop, winding her way through the open land like a giant serpent, her well-trodden path muddy and slow.

Blade was standing by his truck. Joanna, meanwhile, was standing beneath a tree, leaning against the trunk, shoulders hunched as if the weight of the world were on them. His heart leaped on seeing her, but immediately plummeted back down when he realized that something was wrong. Her posture told him so. He wondered if she had received bad news from Dr. Sinclair.

He opened the door to exit the vehicle when he felt Hank's fingers curl around his upper arm. "I'll leave you to make your own way from here," the FBI agent said. "Be careful. I'm almost certain that nobody followed us from Godspeed, but you can never be too cautious. Keep your wits about you."

"Are you leaving already?" Tyler asked, sliding from the seat and onto the frost-hardened ground.

"I have to," Hank replied. "There are a lot of people to contact since Dennison's body was found. But I'll be in touch soon. Stay safe now."

With that, he leaned over and slammed the door shut, before backing out onto the deserted highway and heading away.

Blade was the first to greet Tyler. "Hey, Sheriff," he said, giving him a bear hug. "It's good to see you."

"I think we should get out of here," Tyler said, looking around anxiously. The farmstead was flanked by two small woodlands, a perfect hiding place for attackers. "Who chose this meeting spot?" he asked, pulling his gun from its holster. "You or Hank?"

"I suggested meeting somewhere out of Yardley County, nice and quiet," Blade replied. "But it was Hank who came up with the location." He must have sensed the danger because he asked, "Why? What's wrong?"

But before Tyler could answer, he heard the pop of a gunshot resound through the air, and he instinctively began running to the tree where Joanna stood.

"Joanna!" he yelled. "Get behind the truck. Now!"

TEN

Joanna ignored Tyler's command and reached for her weapon, firing into the trees, where she was certain the shooter was located. Tyler appeared at her side and put his arm around her waist, wrenching her off her feet and carrying her a few yards to drop her onto the ground behind the cover of the truck.

"What are you doing?" he yelled, diving to the ground alongside her. "You left yourself wide open there."

"That's my choice, not yours," she said, scrambling to her knees to look over the hood of the truck. A surge of excitement had gripped her. This was her opportunity to do something useful, something good. If she could isolate the shooter, she could take him down without Tyler or Blade being hurt.

Another shot zinged though the air, hitting the door of the truck. Blade was inside the vehicle, loading his gun with ammunition from the glove box. He crouched low as more bullets peppered the door with alarming frequency.

"I see him," she said, peering into a dense patch of sycamores. She rested her weapon on the hood to steady her aim. But before she could fire, another shooter revealed himself, firing a gun from the opposite side. Joanna managed to fire off just two rounds before being forced to retreat again. The second shooter was firing quickly, giving them no respite from the assault.

Blade tumbled out of the car, holding the weapons bag. "I just saw somebody lay a spike strip on our path out of here," he yelled above the noise. "We can't drive away without every one of our tires being blown."

"Then we hold our ground," Joanna said, reaching inside the gun bag for a semiautomatic shotgun. "How many of them are there?" The firing ceased, and the sudden force of her own voice in the silence took her by surprise. "I see two."

"There are at least four, maybe five," said Blade. "And they're working in formation, coming closer all the time. We're outmanned, outgunned and running out of time."

Tyler pointed to the old farmstead. "Let's get behind the house. We can run through the trees and make for the river. It's our best chance of escape."

Another burst of gunfire hit the truck, piercing the gas tank and sending gasoline trickling onto the frosty earth.

"I'll provide cover for you," Joanna said. She stood and quickly fired off a series of shots. She saw a man heading in their direction, but he quickly retreated under her assault. When she was out of ammunition, she ducked back down and began to reload.

"Joanna, what are you doing?" Tyler said. "The longer we remain behind this truck, the more trapped we'll be. And gasoline is all over the ground. Let's go."

He tugged on her sleeve, but she pulled her arm away. "If I stay here to hold them off, you two can get away." She finished reloading and slipped the barrel back in place. "Quickly. Leave now."

"Deputy Graham," Tyler said, using a voice of commanding force. "You get yourself over to that house right now. And that's an order."

More shots came. It fueled her conviction to be their shield while they escaped. It was the right thing to do in the circumstances. She could be dead in a few months anyway.

She was just about to argue when more shots came and created a spark that ignited the gasoline that had pooled on the ground. The truck quickly caught fire. Flames licked at the metal, sending black smoke swirling into the sky. Tyler grabbed her hand.

"Let's go now!" he shouted.

Joanna knew it was foolish to stay behind a burning truck. She wouldn't be much use as a shield if she was overcome by smoke. She allowed Tyler to pull her up, and she ran as fast as she could to the derelict house. Tyler carried the bag of weapons on his back, and Blade fired shots into the trees as he ran to give them some protection.

Once they were safely behind the house, Joanna searched for a suitable place to hide and provide cover while Tyler and Blade made their escape. Tyler pointed to the river, where a small wooden shape could be seen behind the trees.

"That looks like a boat," he said breathlessly. "Let's head for the water." As if he had already anticipated Joanna's response, he continued. "If you insist on remaining here, Blade and I will be forced to stay with you, and we may all end up getting killed."

She pursed her lips. Tyler had dealt a trump card. She couldn't allow that to happen.

"Okay," she said, gathering her thoughts as a small explosion cast an orange glow on the grass behind Tyler.

"That's the truck going up," Blade said, beginning to head for the river. He moved surprisingly quickly, like an athlete, and was soon far ahead, urging Tyler and Joanna to join him.

Tyler held Joanna's hand tightly, and they sprinted together, weaving through the trees, hearing the sounds of gunfire echo behind them. Joanna could hear the shouts of men pursuing them. Her lungs began to burn. She was wheezing, despite her youth and fitness. This must be a sign of her illness. She was slowing them. But Tyler's firm grip dragged her forward, giving her the extra boost she needed to pick up her pace. She heard Tyler muttering. He was praying. Despite all her doubts about God listening to her words, she did the same.

Blade yelled from up ahead. "Hurry!"

Joanna thought her lungs would burst, but she dug deep and exhausted all her reserves of energy to reach the banks of the river, where a small rowboat was tied to a post. She saw white dots dance across her eyes as dizziness threatened to overwhelm her, but Tyler caught her in his arms and lifted her into the boat before jumping in alongside her. The wooden vessel was weatherworn and rickety, set firm in ice that had formed at the water's edge. It wasn't much to look at, but it was an answer to prayer.

Blade untied the rope while Tyler smashed at the ice surrounding the boat with the oars, allowing them to push out into the free-flowing water. The fog was thick and soon enveloped them, with Tyler powerfully pulling them through the murky water. The shadowy figures of their pursuers could be seen walking up and down the riverbank, searching for them, firing weapons wildly into the mist. Blade positioned himself at the stern and returned fire, making the boat rock wildly with his movement. Joanna felt helpless, recovering from her dizziness and unable to do anything but grip the sides of the boat to give herself stability.

She was thankful when they reached the middle of the river where the current caught the boat, propelling them downstream and well and truly out of sight of their pursuers. Yet Joanna's fear didn't abate. She hated to admit it to herself, but she was terrified. Their boat was small and unstable in this immense body of water, and one sudden shift in movement could turn them over. She wasn't a strong swimmer. She would be swallowed into the cold depths in one quick gulp. She accepted that death would come to her, but not like that. It would be a pointless waste.

She lifted her white knuckles from the sides of the boat and laced her fingers together, bowing her head. God was always the last resort of the desperate, and she certainly fitted that description. She prayed harder than she had ever done, asking for safe passage from this place, for an opportunity to use her remaining time to benefit others and also for forgiveness. She had rejected God too many times, and it pained her deeply.

Yet when she lifted her head, the pain vanished and a sensation of peace descended. The jumble of thoughts in her mind ceased to torment her, having been replaced with a beautiful stillness. As she watched Blade and Tyler steer the boat into a lesser current and take them to the opposite bank, Joanna felt her back straighten, as though a great weight had been lifted from it. Tears of gratitude pricked at her eyes.

God had every right to reject her, to turn His back and let her wallow in the misery that she had created. But in that moment, she knew He had not abandoned her. She felt His presence enveloping her, like a fatherly pair of arms, warm and everlasting.

God had not forsaken her. He was reminding her not to be afraid, to trust his Word and to have faith. And wherever He wanted to lead her, she must be prepared to go willingly.

Tyler dropped to the ground and lay on the grass, breathing hard, letting the soft flakes of newly falling snow fall onto his flushed face. The exertion of rowing, combined with the adrenaline of a narrow escape, had zapped all his energy. They were safe. But for how long?

He sat up. Joanna was kneeling on the ground, sipping from a water bottle he'd handed her a moment ago, her face regaining some of its lost color. Blade had gone to scout out a local farm to see if there was any chance of finding transport. The air around them was silent and incandescent. The mist still hung low, clinging to the river like smoke on a fire, but the increasing wind was slowly whipping it away. The breeze was stinging, and Tyler shifted closer to Joanna, pulling her coat around her tightly.

"You still look a little pale," he said. "That getaway was too close for comfort, huh?"

"It would've been a lot less stressful for you if you'd let me stay at the farmstead and provide cover while you escaped," she said in a flat and emotionless voice. "We almost didn't make it because of me." She put a flat palm on her chest. "My fitness level isn't what it used to be."

"But we *did* make it," he said. "Don't you know me well enough by now to realize that I would never, and I mean *never*, leave anybody behind?"

"I can't expect you to carry me while we search for Mr. X, Tyler." She screwed the top on her water bottle and continued twisting long after the cap was tightened. "It's not fair to you or Blade. If we have to run again, I'll slow you down. We should part ways now, and I'll make my own choices from here on."

Tyler could scarcely believe what she was suggesting.

"Joanna," he said, placing a hand on her cheek. "I'm not leaving you."

She bowed her head and took a deep breath. "My cancer is back."

He said nothing for a few seconds. "I know," he said finally. "I'd already guessed."

She lifted her face to the wind, and small flakes caught in her eyelashes, which she blinked away. "I'm a liability. You should go back to Godspeed, get yourself a good lawyer and prepare your case for court. If the police arrest you again, you'll have even more charges added to the list. I'm guessing you're not even supposed to leave Yardley County."

"I'm well aware of my bail conditions," he said. "And I'm happy to break every single one of them if the reason is justified."

She looked deep into his eyes, imploring him. "But you'll lose your job as sheriff."

He shrugged. "Easy come, easy go."

She stood and began to pace. "But it wasn't easy for you to become our sheriff, Tyler. You worked long and hard to get where you are today. I watched you build up a relationship with the townsfolk, knocking on doors, visiting schools, giving every single person the time of day. You surely remember all these things now, right?"

He nodded. He *did* remember them, and they brought a smile to his face. In a matter of just three days, he had gone from being a reluctant sheriff to loving his job with a passion. His heart belonged in Godspeed, and he was even homesick for it.

"I'm a lost cause now, Tyler," she said. "I don't want to drag you down with me. I love you too much to let that happen..."

"Whoa, hold on a minute." He jumped to his feet. "Let's back up a little bit. What did you just say?"

"I said that I didn't want to drag you down with me."

"No," he said. "What did you say right after that?"

She fell silent.

"Do you love me, Joanna?" he asked quietly. "Did you just say that?"

Her shoulders sagged. She looked defeated. "Yes, I love you, but it doesn't make a difference now—"

He cut her off again. "It makes a difference to *me* because I feel the same way. I've been trying to fight it these last few days, but it just isn't working. I miss you even when you're just in the next room."

She laughed but not happily. "You're only saying that because you don't remember how we used to fight."

"Actually, I *do* remember," he said. "I remember almost everything about you, even that time when I threatened to put you on suspension."

She seemed taken aback. "You said that memories of me were still fuzzy." She took a step away. "You *lied*?"

"Yes, I did," he admitted. "I lied because I wasn't sure if I should stir up old feelings of the past and risk getting burned. But our relationship feels different now." He smiled. "It feels *right*, like we started over on a different foot. I can't stop myself from falling in love with you, and believe me I've tried." He walked to her and tried to draw her near, but she pushed away with a force that almost sent him off balance.

"No, Tyler," she said, raising her voice. "I won't let you sacrifice yourself or your happiness for me. Not only am I placing all of us in serious danger, but there's a tumor inside me that will kill me if the bad guys don't manage to do it first." A tear fell down her face, and she brushed it aside with a quick sweep. "You're young and healthy and you have a bright future ahead. I'll get sicker and sicker as every day passes."

It took Tyler a second or two to gather his thoughts. "I don't want a future without you in it," he said. "I don't care if you get sick and your hair falls out. I don't care if I have to carry you to bed or help you brush your teeth. I don't even care if you have no teeth." He tried to smile, but his throat was tight. "Sorry, that was a bad attempt at a joke."

"I'm not in the mood for jokes," she said, turning to look out over the river and crossing her arms, tucking her hands into her armpits. "I appreciate everything you're saying, Tyler. And if I'm being honest, it makes me love you all the more. You're the most honorable man I ever knew. Even when we fight, I love the fact that you won't abandon your principles. And I know you won't abandon your principles now. So if you won't leave me, then I guess we'll have to go back to Godspeed together. I'll turn myself in and you can get on with your life."

He stood close behind her. He could see Blade in his peripheral vision, making his way across a nearby field, his friend's unique style of walking now instantly recognizable. Placing his hands on Joanna's shoulders, he felt her tense.

"I agree that going home is a good idea for both of us, but please let me keep you out of sight for just a while longer," he said. Truth be told, he couldn't bear the thought of Joanna being taken into custody, where he would be unable to stand by her side, hold her hand, be her rock and support. "We still have one last shot at cracking this case. We have the piece of glass I recovered from the prison with two sets of prints on it. If we can identify who attacked me, we may just find our way to Mr. X. Stay with me until we run those prints through the FBI database. Please."

She didn't turn. "You'll be harboring a wanted fugitive. That's serious."

"Remember what we decided back in Tennessee?" he asked. "We decided not to be afraid."

"I'm not afraid," she said in a small voice. "I'll take whatever's coming, but I don't want to make things worse for you."

Tyler sighed. He wished he could spin her around, gather her up and hold her tight. But her body language told him to keep a good distance.

When Blade appeared next to them, Tyler saw that a wide grin was on his face and a key in his hand.

"I just bought us a new truck," he said. "It's old and rusted and smells of manure, but the engine is good." He looked between his friend and Joanna, clearly sensing the tense atmosphere. "So where do we go from here?"

Tyler and Joanna replied in unison: "Home."

Tyler stoked a good fire in the hearth while Joanna sat in an armchair drinking hot tea and clutching a blanket around her shoulders. She was bathed in the multicolored glow of the Christmas tree lights, looking pensive and lost in thought. It had been an odd sensation to return to a house that had been entirely unfamiliar to him just a few days ago. This time, walking into his home had been like stepping into a comfortable pair of slippers. His simple, rustic home with its shined, wooden floorboards and numerous framed photographs had filled him with a sense of joy. Just as he'd wanted, he was home on Christmas Eve with somebody he loved. But it wasn't the happy ending he'd hoped for.

They had waited until nightfall to return to Godspeed, with Joanna hiding under the bags in case anybody twitched their drapes and caught sight of her. The whole town probably would know by now that Tyler had been arrested and bailed, so they wouldn't be surprised to see him at his home. But Joanna was still a wanted person, and if Crenshaw got a whiff of her presence there, a warrant to search his house would swiftly follow. Tyler wondered how long it would be before the police chief's suspicions were aroused. When the phone rang, Tyler gave a wry smile. It had to be Crenshaw.

He was right.

"Sheriff," Chief Crenshaw said before Tyler even spoke. "I'm glad to hear that you're finally home. I've been calling all day, but you didn't pick up."

Tyler wondered which one of his neighbors had acted as the town gossip.

"Mrs. Yewtree tells me that you have a gentleman friend with you," George continued. "She saw him carrying a heavy bag inside."

Tyler's heart leaped into his throat. The heaviness of the bag had been due to the fact that Joanna was curled up inside.

"That's right," Tyler said. "I have an old SEAL buddy staying with me. That's not against the law, as far as I know."

"From North Carolina, is he?" George asked. "The Tennessee police said they chased a truck with a North Carolina plate out of the Meeman-Shelby Forest State Park yesterday. I'm assuming that this is the same guy."

"You can assume all you like, George," Tyler said stiffly. "But I'm not answering any questions unless you arrest me. This could be interpreted as harassment, you know."

Crenshaw ignored the friendly warning. "You got anybody else staying with you, Sheriff?" he asked. "A young lady perhaps? Petite, beautiful and as hotheaded as a tiger?"

"Joanna's not here. I don't know where she is."

He heard George exhale heavily on the other end of the line. "Maybe your friend in the FBI knows. What's his name again? Hank Carlton?" He exhaled again. The police chief was smoking a cigar. "I know all about Carlton's undercover agent in The Scorpions. His guy turned up dead on the banks of the Mississippi this morning."

Tyler's suspicions were aroused. "What do you know about Agent Dennison?"

"I know that his body was found close to the park," George replied. "And that is right where Joanna was hiding out. She could've been responsible for his murder." He changed his voice to a gentler tone, trying to take a different approach. "I know you're convinced Joanna is innocent, but you're not thinking straight. You took a blow to the head that's messed with all your common sense. You lied to me in the hospital, didn't you, Tyler? You didn't remember me or the mayor at all."

"I admit that I might have exaggerated my recovery," Tyler said. "But I truly do remember everything now. I know Joanna, and she *is* innocent. I'm sure of it."

"Now I *know* you're lying about your memory returning," George said, letting irritation seep through his smooth Southern lilt. "Joanna caused you nothing but trouble since you became sheriff of Yardley. You obviously don't recall how rebellious and disobedient she can be."

"Yes, I do," Tyler said, watching Joanna sip

her drink slowly, snuggled in his favorite brown leather armchair. "And it doesn't matter to me. She has a good heart, and she's learning how to be a better person every day, just like we all are."

Crenshaw snorted in derision, and Tyler began to lose his cool. "I get the feeling that you just plain and simple don't like her," he said hotly.

"No, I don't like her," Crenshaw retorted. "She's always been a snooty one. And once she got her piece of paper from Harvard, she thought she was better than all of us. She reckons she's too good for the likes of me."

Tyler felt realization dawn. "You asked her out on a date, didn't you, George? And she turned you down. That's why you despise her so much."

George fell quiet on the end of the line. Tyler knew he had hit the nail on the head. Chief Crenshaw hated Joanna because she had rejected him.

"Just remember your bail conditions," George said gruffly. "Don't leave the county."

The line went dead, and Tyler hung up the phone, catching sight of the broken frame that he had smashed to pull out the picture of his Dark Skies SEAL buddies. He felt around in his jeans pocket for the folded-up image, taking it out and rubbing his thumb along the crumpled edge. He had nothing but admiration and respect for these five men dressed in desert khakis, rifles strapped to their shoulders, sunglasses shielding them from the glare of the scorching sun and smiles of camaraderie on their faces.

"I know it sounds odd," Blade said, appearing at his side and pointing to the image. "But the Dark Skies mission was the best time of my life. We were shot at, bombed and I even lost a leg. But I've never felt that kind of friendship or excitement since. Sometimes, I'd love to go back, if only for just a day."

"I used to think that, as well," Tyler said, placing the picture on a table. "While my memories were gone, I couldn't ever imagine being happy in this small town. I mean, we're SEALs, right? When danger hits, we're the first ones in and the last ones out. I kept thinking I must've been crazy to leave that kind of life behind."

Blade placed a firm hand on Tyler's shoulder. "So what changed your mind?" He cast a glance at Joanna. She was fighting to keep sleep at bay, her eyelids drooping languidly in the warmth of the fire. "Or is it pretty obvious?"

"Special Forces is a younger man's life," Tyler said. "I realized that God doesn't want me to fight wars my whole life. There are so many other things to experience."

"Such as?" Blade asked.

"The simple things in life are usually the best," he replied. "Sharing a meal with family, taking a walk on Main Street, swimming with kids in the lake on a summer's day..." He tailed off.

He didn't have the heart to continue speaking about a life that he wasn't sure he would ever have. If Joanna was determined to shut him out, then he would need to take a long while to accept it and move on. By the time he was ready to date again, he may be another ten years older.

Blade removed his hand from Tyler's shoulder. "Well, before you start planning the rest of your life, we'd better finish the investigation we started. Joanna can't stay here forever, and we're almost out of options. We have to run the prints on the glass from the prison as soon as possible. It's our last hope of uncovering the identity of someone who can lead us to Mr. X." He cocked his head to the side. "Who knows? Those prints could even belong to Mr. X himself."

Tyler had already been thinking along the same lines, but his attention was caught by the melodic strains of "Hark the Herald Angels Sing". He went to the front window and pulled back the drapes. "We have carolers. They're from the local church."

"Somebody might be hiding among them," Blade said. "We shouldn't answer."

But Tyler didn't agree. The joyful sound of Christmas was welcome and reminded him to take comfort in God's promise. There was no way Tyler would let these carolers pass by without allowing their song to uplift and revitalize his flagging spirits. He walked over to Joanna to see that she had fallen fast asleep, blanket tucked firmly under her chin. He pushed her chair into the corner of the room where she would be undetectable to anybody on the porch. She murmured but didn't wake, and he then joined Blade at the front door, reaching into his pocket for some money to donate.

"Tyler," Blade said. "I don't think you understand the urgency we're facing. We probably only have a matter of hours before Joanna's presence is detected here. We don't have time to waste."

"It's not a waste of time to pause for a moment of reflection on Christmas Eve," Tyler said, turning the knob and opening the door to reveal a throng of faces standing on his snowy porch. "I need this."

Then he stopped speaking, gave the singers his full attention and enjoyed the calm before the storm.

Joanna woke with a start and threw the blanket to the floor. It took her a few seconds to recognize the white-walled room with its numerous framed photographs and SEAL memorabilia. With a sigh of relief, she realized that she was in Tyler's house. She was safe.

She checked the clock. It was approaching 1:00 a.m. She could hear Tyler and Blade talking in whispered tones in the kitchen. Although she couldn't make out the words, she detected anxiety in their voices. She stood and stretched, instantly sitting back down again as she felt the dizziness of rising too quickly. Her movement alerted Tyler, and he walked into the dark living room, switching on a lamp as he passed.

"I wanted to let you rest," he said quietly. "You were exhausted."

Joanna rubbed the sleep from her eyes. The wood on the fire had charred away to embers, white hot and flaky. She felt as burned out as the ash. Where a fire had once been stoked in her belly, she was now empty and spent. She knew that Tyler's arms curling around her would give her the comfort she needed, but she couldn't bring herself to ask. There was no point.

She flicked her eyes to the clock on the mantel. "It's Christmas Day."

He walked to her, smiling, and planted a kiss on her forehead. "Merry Christmas, Joanna." She shrank from his affection, and Tyler's smile faded. "Blade and I were just discussing a plan to visit the sheriff's office and run the prints from the glass through the FBI's Fingerprint Identification System."

"What if there's no match?" she asked. "I guess it's the end of the road."

"Not exactly," he replied. "If we don't get a hit, we can hand the glass over to the feds for DNA testing."

"But it's the end of the road for me, right?" she said "Without a new lead, there are no more avenues of investigation. I'll have to turn myself in."

Tyler nodded. "Yes, but let's not get ahead of ourselves until we get the job done."

Joanna pushed herself out of the chair. Her limbs were weary, but she hid this fact from Tyler by forcing a spring into her step. "Are we leaving right away?"

He rubbed his neck uncomfortably. "I kind of assumed you would stay here while Blade and I go." He pointed to the window. "It's snowing out, and it's no place for…" He stopped.

"For a sick woman," she said, crossing her arms.

He came close to her, placing his hands on her shoulders. His palms seemed to create a burning sensation on her skin, and she twined her fingers together like a teenager on a first date. She hated the way Tyler made her feel, yet she craved it.

"You can't pretend you're not sick," he said. "*I* can't pretend you're not sick. I'd do absolutely anything to make you well again. I would walk over hot coals for you. But I can't make your cancer disappear, so all I can do is keep you warm and dry and safe."

Her heart fluttered. Hearing him talk like this made her feel as if her life had true value, as if her diseased body had a right to be loved. But it was a fleeting sensation, as she remembered what lay ahead—a hospital bed, chemotherapy, drips, monitors, heartache. And at the end of it all, a coffin was likely to be awaiting her.

"I'm not made of glass, Tyler," she said, lifting her head. "So please don't treat me like I'm fragile. I've been with you every step of the way until now, and I'm not about to let some cancer cells stop me from seeing this through to the end." She knew she was getting through to him. If there was one thing that appealed to Tyler, it was mental toughness, and she had it in spades. "I deserve to be part of this final push to discover the truth."

He smiled. Since returning home, he had showered and shaved, revealing his baby-faced dimples once again.

"I'll go see if I can find you some warmer clothes," he said, looking down at her jeans. "Wrap up well and eat something before we go. Blade made soup."

"Great," she said, brushing past him to head for the kitchen.

He caught her by the arm. "Whatever happens

tonight, I want you to get out safely. Do you understand what I'm saying?"

She understood perfectly. "You're asking me not to take any undue risks, right?"

"Exactly." The pressure applied by his fingers on her forearm was gentle, yet insistent. "I don't want you to take any bullets for anybody. Our lives are all worth the same." His eyes looked to be collecting moisture. "Don't be a hero, Joanna. Please."

She uttered the only words that Tyler would accept. "I won't." But she stopped short of making a promise.

She continued her path into the kitchen and busied herself, acutely aware of Tyler's eyes resting on her, no doubt trying to gauge whether she was telling the truth. She gave nothing away, yet a shiver of trepidation traveled the length of her body. She somehow knew that a sinister force was lurking close by, placing the three of them in mortal danger. They could soon be staring death in the face.

And when that happened, she fully intended to be Tyler's hero.

ELEVEN

The sheriff's office was on the edge of town, positioned between the fire station and an antiques store. It was a grand, gray brick building, with tall windows and the date of its incorporation etched into a limestone block above the door: 1842.

The gleaming white frames on the windows were instantly recognizable to Tyler, and he found a flood of fond memories returning. He and his two deputies enjoyed a way of life that many would envy, characterized by good neighbors, loyal citizens and a community spirit that left nobody out. Policing Yardley County was easy compared to most, as violence was rare in their sleepy towns. The Scorpions had been the most serious criminal activity that the county had ever seen, or would ever be likely to see again.

The walk to the sheriff's office had been the most peaceful of Tyler's life, the falling snow descending from the black sky like confetti, covering their footprints almost as soon as they appeared. Godspeed had never looked more beautiful to him than on that white Christmas Eve, shimmering like a jewel in the crown of Yardley County. The three friends positioned themselves to the side of the building, close to the door, ducking behind a wall. Tyler had struggled to find them all suitably light colored clothing as perfect camouflage for the weather, but he had managed to outfit everyone in white or gray items, including woolen hats. Joanna was wearing his old skiing pants, secured with a belt, and a puffy jacket that made her look like a giant marshmallow. The wind had just started to pick up. A heavy snowstorm was brewing, and he knew that their return journey would be tough. He was glad they dressed for the drop in temperature.

"How do we get in?" Joanna asked in a whisper. "You must have a plan."

Tyler pulled his office keys from his pocket. He figured that he may as well try the simplest option first.

"*That's* your plan?" she said incredulously. "City hall must've changed the locks surely?"

He scuttled over to the door. "There's only one way to find out."

He slipped the key into the heavy-duty lock on the front door and turned it. He heard the familiar clunk of the bolt sliding from its casing, and the door opened with a gentle tug.

Tyler waited for the bleep of the security alarm to start up, but no sound came. It looked like security procedures had gone awry since he'd been away. Under the circumstances of his sudden departure, the locks ought to have been changed and the security alarm set every night, yet neither had been done. But he couldn't stay irritated for long, as city hall's incompetence was their good fortune.

Blade and Joanna followed him inside and locked the door behind them. The office was bitterly cold, with moonlight settled on the three desks and paper trays. Tyler's desk was exactly as he had left it on that day he had rushed to Joanna's aid at the prison: tidy, organized and polished. If only he could compartmentalize his love for Joanna in the same way he filed his paperwork. His heartache would be so much easier to bear if he could box it off.

Come on, Sheriff, he thought. *Keep your mind on the job.*

Despite the tidiness of his desk, the filing cabinets were in disarray, drawers left open and papers hanging out of their folders. The shelves were in a similar state, disorganized, untidy and showing evidence of having been rifled through.

"Look at this place," Tyler said angrily. "It's a total mess."

"Let's not worry about that for now," Joanna said, walking to his computer and switching it on. "We should focus on the job at hand."

A dingy glow from the computer lit up the room, and Tyler quickly navigated to the FBI's fingerprint database, feeling his pulse quicken as he input the login details. Would a block have been placed on his access code? Would he now be announcing his presence at the station to the authorities?

With a feeling of trepidation, he waited for the database to load, placing the prints on the scanner in readiness. When the computer displayed a "scan in progress" message, he breathed a sigh of relief.

"We're in," he said. "It usually takes twenty-five to thirty minutes to run through all possible matches. Let's keep our eyes and ears open while we wait. I know it's deserted outside, but—"

He stopped midsentence as a noise caused him to freeze to the spot. A clinking sound was coming from behind the door that led to the sheriff department's two jail cells. It was a secure place to hold people for short periods of time, usually drunks needing to sleep it off. He had assumed the cells would be empty. The station closed at 7:00 p.m. on Christmas Eve every year, and one deputy remained on call in case of emergency. The whole town shut down for Christmas Day, so patrolling officers and deputies were given time off to spend with their families.

"Luke would never leave a prisoner unattended, would he?" Tyler asked Joanna quietly.

"Never," she replied.

He pulled out his gun. "Well, somebody's there. Let's check it out."

He then turned to Blade. "Stay here and make sure the fingerprint process runs through correctly."

"Sure thing," Blade replied, going to stand by the computer in the corner, gun in hand. "I'll be ready."

"Let's go carefully," Tyler said to Joanna, as he saw the look of zeal on her face, and old worries about her recklessness bubbled to the surface. "Absolutely no shooting unless necessary, okay?"

She gave a quick nod, and, with fear in his heart, he began to walk slowly forward. The fear, however, was not for his own safety. It was for hers.

Joanna stayed close behind her sheriff as he approached the door that led to the station's jail cells. They were rarely used, and no prisoner was allowed to remain in a cell overnight without a deputy present.

Tyler reached for the handle and turned it slowly. Joanna's heart thudded as she kept her finger hovering over the trigger of her weapon. Throwing the door open wide, Tyler assumed the defensive position, legs wide, gun raised, calling out an order to put hands in the air.

The face that greeted them was thin and gaunt, with sunken eyes. It was Tommy, standing behind the bars, his bony fingers curled around the metal. He looked startled to see them and visibly jumped in shock.

"Tommy!" Tyler exclaimed, "What are you doing here?"

Tommy flashed his familiar gummy smile. "Well, I'm not having a happy holiday, that's for sure. I'm hiding from The Scorpions."

Joanna holstered her weapon and walked to the cell, while Tyler called out the all clear to Blade. She touched Tommy's fingers. They were icy.

"I thought you were in FBI custody," she said. "Crenshaw told Tyler that an agent came to take you away. What happened to you, Tommy? Why did you go to Crenshaw for help in the first place? And how did you end up here, alone?"

Tommy's eyes moved back and forth anxiously as he spoke. "When I got back to Godspeed after visiting you in Tennessee, I noticed I was being tailed by The Dentist."

Joanna glanced at Tyler. "Yeah," she said. "We heard."

Tommy moistened his lips, his tongue darting like a lizard's over the cracked skin. "Everybody's terrified of The Dentist. There's only one reason he tails people—to kill them. I didn't even bother going home. I drove straight to Godspeed police station and asked for protection."

"Did you really think that Crenshaw was the best person to protect you?" Tyler asked. "You said yourself that Dennison suspected he was Mr. X."

"That's why I figured he wouldn't do anything stupid," Tommy replied. "If I'd died while in his custody, he'd have a whole heap of questions to answer. Besides which, when you're being tailed by The Dentist, you don't have a lot of time to escape. The police station was the closest place to go."

"So what did Crenshaw do?" Joanna asked.

"He contacted the FBI's Organized Crime Unit to come take me away. An agent named Hank Carlton turned up the next day and took me to a safe house in some fancy suburb of Memphis. He's Dennison's handler, but I never met him before. From what Dennison said, I don't think he liked me much."

The mention of Hank got Tyler's full attention. "Hank didn't say any of this to me when I saw him this morning. Was he alone when he came to get you from the police station?"

"Yeah," Tommy said. "And something didn't feel right. I just didn't trust the guy, you know? He's kinda creepy, and the safe house was deserted. Nobody else there at all. As soon as his back was turned, I ran and thumbed a ride back to Godspeed."

"Why did you come back to Godspeed?" Joanna asked. "Surely this is the last place on Earth you want to be."

Tommy shrugged. "I got no place else to go. I'm scared, man. I don't trust Crenshaw, I don't trust Hank Carlton, and I wouldn't last five minutes on the run from The Scorpions. The only people I trust are you guys, but I didn't know where to find you, so I went to Deputy Hutchence and begged him to hide me." He looked around the cold, bare cell. "And he let me stay here."

"*Luke* let you stay here unsupervised!" Tyler exclaimed. "Nobody is allowed to stay in a locked cell without a deputy present. You'd be trapped if there was a fire." He rubbed his forehead. "I never knew Luke could be so stupid."

"Don't be too hard on him," Tommy said, pushing the cell door to show that it was unlocked. "He only agreed to hide me over the holidays, just until I figure out what to do. He didn't want to toss me out into the snow at Christmastime."

He touched the cross around his neck. "Even Mary and Joseph were given a stable, right?"

"I'm sure Luke thought he was being a Good Samaritan, but you *can't* stay here," Tyler said. "We'll help you get someplace safe."

Joanna opened the cell door. "A cold, bare jail cell is no place for anybody to spend Christmas Day. Leave with us and we'll look after you."

Just then, an excited shout went up from the main office. It was Blade.

"I got a match," he called. "It's Hank Carlton."

Tyler rushed into the office and gazed at the computer screen in disbelief. The smiling photograph of Hank Carlton was staring back at him.

"The two sets of prints on the glass belong to you and Hank," Blade said. "All those times when Hank was pretending to help us, he was just trying to lead us into a trap. Every time he showed up, trouble seemed to follow."

"He even murdered one of his own men to throw us off track," Tyler said, realizing how close they had come to being killed by Hank. "He was one of The Scorpions gunmen at the park in Tennessee, but when the police showed up, he had to come up with a plan to direct us to his safe house in Germantown. I don't doubt we'd be dead by now if we hadn't left that place so quickly. No wonder he was jittery, checking his watch. He was waiting for more gang members to show up."

Joanna's face showed that she clearly struggled to comprehend this information. "But he saved us by killing the sniper in the woods." She shook her head as an obvious thought must have occurred to her. "Hank didn't kill the sniper. Hank *was* the sniper, right?"

"Exactly," Tyler said. "Once the police showed up, he couldn't run the risk of his accomplice being arrested and questioned. So he killed him, and pretended to be the hero."

"I knew there was something bad about him," Tommy said, fidgeting nervously next to Tyler. "I knew."

"Tommy," Tyler said, turning to him. "Do you know why Agent Dennison might have wanted to frame Chief Crenshaw? Those photos he gave you of Crenshaw outside the prison were faked. It looks like somebody wanted to throw us off the scent."

"Dennison told me that he took those photos personally," Tommy replied. "I had no reason to distrust him." A look of surprise flashed over his face. "Maybe Dennison and Hank were in it together. But Hank got greedy and wanted his agent's share, too. So he killed him."

"Well," Blade said, raising his gun. "It looks like we'll be able to ask Hank for all the answers personally, because he just pulled into the parking lot."

Tyler spun on his heel to watch Hank's black SUV come slowly into the lot, leaving tire tracks on the smooth, powdery ground. The distinctive white stripes on the paintwork identified it unmistakably as Hank's vehicle.

"How did he know we were here?" Joanna exclaimed.

"He might have set up an alert on the fingerprint database to give him the heads-up if I ever accessed it," Tyler said. "And he obviously stayed close to Godspeed to be ready to launch another attack." He pulled Joanna over to the window. "You should take Tommy back to my place while Blade and I deal with Hank."

He suspected her reaction would be fierce, and he wasn't wrong. "No," she said, pushing him away. "That's not fair."

Tyler could see Hank's taillights glowing red in the haze of the snowstorm as he parked. "Tommy is in grave danger here," he said. "He's a civilian, and we have a duty to protect him."

Joanna's breathing became shallow and rapid, as though she were panicking. "But what about you?" she said breathlessly. "I have a duty to protect *you*."

The taillights cut out and the door of Hank's

SUV opened. A shadowy figure, hunched against the wind, emerged from the vehicle.

Tyler opened the window in a corner of the office, and a blast of snow hit him full in the face. "I know you want to be a hero, Joanna, but heroes don't always face the bullets." He snapped his fingers, indicating for Tommy to jump through the window. "Heroes also guide people to safety. Tommy needs you."

Joanna's face showed its conflicted emotions. She was obviously torn. "Okay, okay," she relented. "I'll take care of Tommy."

The shaking meth addict didn't need any further instruction. He scrambled onto the frame and dropped into a snowdrift beneath. Tyler could see Hank moving closer and closer to the door of the station. He lifted Joanna off her feet and maneuvered her into the frosty night. As she swung her legs through the window, she jerked her body around, clung onto Tyler with ferocious strength and kissed him hard on the lips.

"I love you, Tyler," she said quickly. "I have to say it, just in case."

He smiled. "I'll be fine. I'm not about to get myself killed."

Joanna jumped from the window ledge, landing next to Tommy. "I know," she said, pushing herself to stand. "I'm saying it just in case anything happens to me."

She then grabbed Tommy's arm, yanked him from the drift and disappeared into the whiteout.

Tyler closed the window, secured it and then went to stand with Blade. They raised their guns and trained them on the front door, waiting to see what Hank had in store for them. Would he be aware of the fingerprint match they found on the database? Would he now know the game was over? Would he blast through the locked door with a powerful weapon? They simply didn't know. But they were ready for anything.

The last thing Tyler expected was for Hank to calmly unlock the door with a key and step into the station, a thermal coffee cup in hand, stamping his feet on the mat.

"So what did you find?" the agent said, bending to pull compacted snow from the treads of his shoes. "Don't tell me you came up empty again—"

He stopped abruptly as he lifted his head and realized he was staring down the barrels of two guns. He dropped the metal cup, and hot coffee splashed across the carpet, sending steam rising into the air. The color drained from his face, and he staggered backward, wide-eyed and open-mouthed.

It was clear that Hank had been expecting to see somebody else waiting to greet him.

"How come you have a key for my station,

Hank?" Tyler asked. "And who exactly were you expecting to find here tonight?"

In his head the word *no* repeated over and over. Had he just made the biggest mistake of his life?

"You were expecting to see Tommy, weren't you?" Tyler said. "You're working together, looking for evidence to destroy."

Hank continued to stare, dumbstruck. "I…I… think I need a lawyer," he stammered.

The more Tyler thought about recent events, the clearer the facts became. Tommy had gone to ask Crenshaw for protection in order to gain access to the two police stations in Godspeed. He'd no doubt managed to make copies of Crenshaw's keys, so he could trawl through paperwork at his leisure and find out exactly what Yardley County's law enforcement agencies had uncovered about The Scorpions and Mr. X. Luke hadn't allowed Tommy to stay in the cells; Tommy had simply walked into the station using his own key. He had conned them all with his flaky, meth addict persona. And Hank had been his trusted sidekick, protecting him from those who sought his true identity. All this time, they had pretended not to know each other well, yet they were coordinating attacks, trying to make sure all three friends were killed in one hit.

Tyler looked at the window, through which Joanna had just disappeared. "Tommy is Mr. X," he gasped, slapping a hand to his face. "Oh no, what have I done?"

What better cover was there for the leader of a notorious criminal gang than a scared, wide-eyed informant? Dennison had been sucked in, and he had been played like a piano before being brutally murdered. Tommy hadn't gone to Tennessee to help Joanna unmask Mr. X. He had gone to scope out their hiding place and set-up, trying to lure them to Germantown with faked evidence. Had they decided to go to the safe house, they would no doubt have been faced with a team of assassins, ready to dispose of them cleanly and quietly instead of risking a public shootout in the state park. When Blade took away Tommy's cell phone that night, The Scorpions' leader had been prevented from changing the plan until the following day, when Hank had launched his attack. It was all so clear now, like mist evaporating to reveal a horrifying scene.

But worse than all of this was the fact that he had sent Joanna out into the dark night with the man who wanted her dead.

"Stay with Hank," Tyler said to Blade. "I gotta go."

He roughly pushed past the corrupt FBI agent, knocking him hard into the wall. Then he burst through the front door, set his face against the rising wind and ran with all his might into the deserted street.

* * *

Joanna battled against the storm that was increasingly in intensity. The snow was driving hard into her chest, and she bowed her head, concentrating on breathing steadily. Every child would now be tucked in bed, their stockings hung on the mantel, awaiting the arrival of the big day. It was a million miles away from her situation.

Tommy was lagging behind, and she stopped to wait. Despite her belief that her fitness level was low, Tommy's seemed to be even worse, and he needed to rest every few paces. She wondered whether he might suddenly keel over in the snow. What would she do then?

"Let's take a break here for a while," Tommy said, pointing to a bus stop with an enclosed shelter.

Joanna shook her head. "I know you're tired, Tommy, but giving up is the very worst thing you can do in situations like this. Dig deep and keep going."

As she willed him to continue moving, she looked at the virgin snow lying on the ground, heavily etched with two sets of footprints: hers and Tommy's. She imagined her continued journey to Tyler's home, perhaps creating just one set of prints, as she might be forced to carry Tommy on her back. Watching him struggle onward, she knew with certainty that she would be prepared to do this for him. She would summon all her reserves of energy and lift him onto her shoulders rather than leave him in the cold. And as she thought these words, she remembered the footprints in the sand. If she was prepared to carry a man through a storm, then surely she could accept that God would lovingly carry her across the sand. It gave her hope and strength at the exact moment she needed them most.

"Come on, Tommy," she urged. "Lean on me for support."

As Tommy approached, her cell phone began to buzz in her pocket, and she pulled it out, holding it in her gloved hand. It was Tyler. When she answered, she could barely understand him. The weather must be affecting the signal and he sounded breathless, as if he was sprinting.

She managed to make out the words. "Danger…get out…run."

"Slow down, Tyler," she said, slipping the cell under her hat to hear more clearly. "Who's in danger?"

"You!"

She heard the reply loud and clear, but it was too late. Bony fingers curled around her mouth, forcing her to drop the cell into the snow as she struggled to break free.

She tried to twist her body to see her attacker, convinced that a stalker had appeared from the snowy night, but to her horror, she saw that her assailant was Tommy. His sinewy, scrawny body suddenly didn't seem so weak, and his grip was powerful. His previous expression of timidity and fear was now replaced with steeliness, his eyes growing hard and intense like a man determined to win.

"Tommy, what are you doing?" she managed to splutter.

"What does it look like I'm doing?" he said, tightening his fingers around her neck. "I'm killing you." He spoke with unrestrained fury. "How dare you infiltrate *my* organization and attempt to destroy everything I've worked so hard to achieve? I had really high hopes for you, Joanna. Your betrayal cut me deep." He brought his face close to hers. "I despise you almost as much as I despised Dennison."

Joanna felt her vision fade as blackness edged around her line of sight. She scraped her nails over Tommy's face, not quite believing this was happening. Her fingers caught the chain around his neck, on which the cross dangled. It broke in her hand and flew through the air.

"I'm glad to be rid of that," Tommy said with a snarling tone. "But it served a purpose for a while." He smiled. "It's amazing how much you can get away with when you pretend to be one of God's children." He narrowed his eyes, loosening his fingers for a few seconds. "Crenshaw wasn't fooled though. I had a tough job getting hold of his keys to copy them." Joanna gasped for breath as Tommy squeezed her throat with force. "But I did it eventually. I always get what I want in the end."

"No," Joanna croaked, pulling at Tommy's clenched fingers with her own. How was he so strong? She thought meth was meant to make people progressively weaker, but he was much tougher than he looked.

Tommy obviously noticed her scanning his body, searching for a weak spot. "Don't let my lack of muscles fool you." He laughed. "Appearances can be deceptive. I gave up meth years ago. You'd be surprised how healthy I am now." His voice faded with her consciousness. "Stop fighting, Joanna. Just let go."

Tommy repeated these last three words again: *Just let go*, willing her to stop struggling. And it stirred something fierce inside her. She didn't want to let go. She didn't want to die. She wanted to fight. Not only did she want to defeat Tommy, but she wanted to defeat her cancer, and with God's grace, she would do both.

She imagined that Tommy's fingers were gripping her in the same way as her cancer cells: firm, unrelenting, terrifying. And it made her mad. She would not allow herself to be taken without putting up the most ferocious fight of her life. Summoning all her energy, she balled her hands into fists and began wildly throwing punches in the air, some connecting with Tommy's face, others catching nothing but falling snow.

Tommy was taken aback at the suddenness of Joanna's renewed defense, and he tried to reposition his hands to give him a tighter hold. The quick moment of respite allowed her to take a deep gulp of air and feed oxygen to her weary body.

"I...will...never...let...go," she said between breaths. "Not for anything."

She pulled her foot from the ground, her knee connecting with Tommy's groin forcefully. He yelped in pain, doubling over and clutching his belly. She turned to run, but he yanked the fabric of her coat, sending her tumbling backward into the powdery snow. She and Tommy grappled with each other, rolling along the sidewalk, being buffeted by the wind, vying for the upper hand.

Then she heard Tyler's voice. It was loud, strong and authoritative, calling her name, ordering Tommy to back off. She had never felt such love for the sheriff as she did at that moment. Not only was he safe, but he had come to her aid.

The pressure of Tommy's body on top of hers was eased, and she saw him being lifted high into the air, his face contorted and pained. Then he was unceremoniously dumped into the snow before Tyler's knee was planted in the small of his back and cuffs placed on his wrists.

She heard Tyler say, "Tommy Roper, I am arresting you for…" Then he stopped, as a police car appeared on the road, making its way to their location as quickly as it dared through the treacherous conditions. "Never mind," he continued. "I'll let somebody else deal with you. I've got a more important person to check on."

Deputy Hutchence jumped from the cruiser at the curbside, surveying the scene. "Your friend Blade called me from the station. He said there was an emergency. I'm on my way there now, but it looks like you need some help here, sir."

Tommy kicked his legs in petulant anger, shouting and cussing.

"Put him in the cruiser," Tyler said. "And take him to the sheriff's office. Blade can explain everything. Joanna and I will follow you back after a few minutes."

Joanna watched Luke yank Tommy up from the ground and roughly push him into the back of the cruiser. But she didn't sit up. She was so very tired and continued to lie on her back in the soft cushion of snow, blinking slowly as the white flakes swirled around her face. Her tussle with Tommy had taken its toll. Her legs were heavy and her breathing was rapid. But she was alive and it felt good. The shock of almost being killed so senselessly had jolted her senses back to reality.

Tyler gently lifted her into his arms. "You okay?"

"Yeah," she replied. "But I'm still in a state of shock." The flashing lights became fuzzy as the cruiser headed down the street. "Did Tommy Roper really fool everybody so easily? I feel like such an idiot."

"You weren't an idiot," he said. "None of us spotted it. Besides, you did a great job of subduing him. I don't think I really needed to step in."

She knew he was being kind. If he hadn't intervened when he did, the outcome could have been fatal for her. "I wanted to be your hero tonight," she said quietly. "But you ended up being mine."

He strode into the shelter of the bus stop and lowered her to her feet. Then he pulled the hood of her coat tightly around her face and held her close in his arms. "There's more than one way to be a hero, you know."

"I think I realize that now." She looked at the footprints in the snow. "I always equated strength with physical ability, and the thought of becoming frail horrified me." She let her gaze return to Tyler's unmoving eyes. "I thought it was a weakness to let God carry me, but I now see that it's the most empowering thing I can do. A true hero knows which battles are worth fighting, and I've been fighting the wrong ones."

He slipped a finger inside her hood and held it open an inch. Then he brought his lips close to her ear, his breath warm and tickly on her skin. "True heroes battle cancer like a boss," he whispered. "And that's a fact."

She smiled. "I'm not gonna argue that point."

Joanna knew she was ready for that particular battle, but she wasn't sure about Tyler. He had no idea just how sick she would become, and she didn't want to trap him into a relationship based on sympathy or obligation.

He clearly understood the thoughts running through her mind. "I love you, Joanna," he said, pulling her as close as possible. "Nothing will change that, I promise."

He put his hand in his pocket and pulled out a sprig of mistletoe. "Now," he said, holding the twig above his head. "I think we should celebrate Christmas Day in traditional style. What do you say?"

She let out a spluttering laugh. "Where did you get that?"

He raised an eyebrow. "I keep it with me in case of emergency. You never know when the perfect opportunity might arise."

"I guess this *would* seem like the perfect opportunity," she said teasingly. "But I'm still wondering where you got the mistletoe."

He rolled his eyes. "Aw, come on. What does a guy have to do to get a kiss from the woman he loves?"

"Absolutely nothing," she replied, tugging off her gloves with her teeth and cupping his face in her hands. "I'm a sure thing."

Against the beautiful backdrop of a snow-covered Godspeed, she pressed her lips onto his and thanked God for the blank, white canvas that lay out before her, unblemished in its purity and ready to receive a brand-new set of footprints.

EPILOGUE

Tyler positioned a gold star on top of the decorated tree and stood back to admire his work. He had waited until Christmas Eve to decorate the tree, as the day held extra significance. Today had been Joanna's final session of chemotherapy. After almost twelve months of grueling treatment, her cancer was in remission and her prognosis couldn't be better. And Tyler was on top of the world.

Joanna came to stand next to him. "Not bad," she said. "I always knew you were the artistic type."

He placed an arm around her shoulders and kissed the top of her head. She had tied a brightly colored scarf around her scalp, hiding her hair loss, and the colors of orange, yellow and pink suited her sunny smile perfectly. She looked tired and a little gaunt, but utterly beautiful.

"You remember the blizzard we had last Christmas Eve?" she asked.

Tyler laughed. "How could I forget? It was the best day of my life. I got to kiss you for the first time."

She jerked her head toward the window. "Do you think we'll see a repeat of the same conditions this year?"

He looked out over his yard where a flurry of snow had started to fall. Already, his lawn was liberally dusted like a Christmas cake.

"As long as we don't see a repeat of the same *events* as last year, then I'll be happy," he said. "I'm expecting a much calmer Christmas this year."

With Hank Carlton and Tommy Roper both awaiting trial in a high-security federal facility, The Scorpions activity had diminished to almost nothing, and Yardley County was free of the scourge of crystal meth. Hank had cut a deal with the prosecutor early on, admitting that Joanna had been framed by the gang and stating that Tommy had ordered the murder of Agent Liam Dennison. Hank would now be assured of a long custodial sentence, but Tommy would be unlikely to ever taste freedom again. Tyler, meanwhile, was back to being Yardley County's well-loved, baby-faced sheriff.

"I'm glad to be mostly writing traffic tickets and helping old ladies cross the street these days," he said. "I prefer the quiet life."

"I'm looking forward to getting back to work myself," Joanna said with a sigh. "I'd like to help a few old ladies cross the street, too."

He turned her body to his and hugged her tightly. "You'll be back on the job soon enough. Everybody wants you back on the team but not before you're ready." He pulled away to give her an enormous smile. "Even Chief Crenshaw and Mayor Landon have become your biggest fans. They've put your name forward for a commendation award."

"No way!" she exclaimed, furrowing the line where her eyebrows had previously been. "That's a surprise."

"Talking of surprises," he said, releasing his grip and reaching down to the carpet beneath the tree. "I thought you might like to open this now." He handed her a small, beautifully wrapped box, complete with a satin ribbon, curled into perfect spirals.

A knot grew in his stomach. Would she guess what was inside? Was it too soon to ask the question?

She took the gift from his hand and flashed a grin. "Store wrapping?"

He laughed. "You got me."

He watched her run her eyes over the paper, teasing it around the edges. "Is this what I think it is? It feels like a ring box."

He nodded, his mouth dry, his breath shallow. He assumed the position and dropped to a bended knee, hand on heart. But the words refused to come. For the first time in his whole life, he was choked up. Everything he had planned to say went right out the window and he was mute.

"Oh Tyler," she said, reaching out to stroke his face. "My answer is yes."

He rose, lifted her off her feet and swung her around in a circle. He still couldn't find his voice in all the emotion, so he pressed his mouth onto hers and decided that actions spoke louder than words.

* * * * *

If you liked this story, pick up these other
NAVY SEAL DEFENDERS *books*
by Elisabeth Rees:

Bound by honor and dedicated to protection.

LETHAL EXPOSURE
FOUL PLAY
COVERT CARGO

Available now from Love Inspired Suspense!

Find more great reads at
www.LoveInspired.com

Dear Reader,

Thank you for sharing in Tyler and Joanna's story in this fourth installment of the Navy SEAL Defenders miniseries. If you enjoyed getting to know the character of Blade, then I hope you will join me for his story (coming soon), which will be the fifth and final book of the series.

I have always loved the poem "Footprints in the Sand," as it perfectly illustrates how God's care of us is strongest when we are at our weakest. After Joanna's cancer diagnosis, she rails against God and turns from Him, believing that He has abandoned her. Yet, it is during this darkest time that God carries her. She refuses to see it, but the signs of His love are present in her life. And Tyler points out perhaps the most important of these signs when he says to Joanna, "You're still alive." By simply waking up each morning, we are experiencing God's grace, particularly if we are battling a serious illness or injury.

Despite Tyler's amnesia, his faith in God is unshakeable and unforgettable. Tyler's strength and dependability draw Joanna close, and she allows him to see the emotional pain that she has stored up for many years. This connection allows them to develop an intimacy that has previously eluded them. Tyler's lack of memory means he is now a blank canvas, and they can start over on a new page. I think we could all benefit from a bit of memory loss sometimes. When another person has hurt our feelings or behaved badly, it can affect the way we treat them, even though we have forgiven them. When Tyler remembered nothing of Joanna, he did not judge her on her past actions, and their relationship flourished because of it.

Only by truly forgetting past discretions can we move forward in newness. It is easier said than done, but with God's grace we can forget what lies behind and strain forward to what lies ahead.

Blessings,
Elisabeth

LARGER-PRINT BOOKS!

GET 2 FREE LARGER-PRINT NOVELS PLUS 2 FREE MYSTERY GIFTS

Love Inspired®

Larger-print novels are now available...

REQUEST YOUR FREE BOOKS!
2 FREE WHOLESOME ROMANCE NOVELS
IN LARGER PRINT
PLUS 2
FREE
MYSTERY GIFTS

※※※※※※※※※※※※※※※※※※※※※※※※※※

HEARTWARMING™

※※※※※※※※※※※※※※※※※※※※※※※※※※

Wholesome, tender romances

YES! Please send me 2 FREE Harlequin® Heartwarming Larger-Print novels and my 2 FREE mystery gifts (gifts worth about $10). After receiving them, if I don't wish to receive any more books, I can return the shipping statement marked "cancel." If I don't cancel, I will receive 4 brand-new larger-print novels every month and be billed just $5.24 per book in the U.S. or $5.99 per book in Canada. That's a savings of at least 19% off the cover price. It's quite a bargain! Shipping and handling is just 50¢ per book in the U.S. and 75¢ per book in Canada.* I understand that accepting the 2 free books and gifts places me under no obligation to buy anything. I can always return a shipment and cancel at any time. Even if I never buy another book, the two free books and gifts are mine to keep forever.

161/361 IDN GHX2

Name	(PLEASE PRINT)	
Address		Apt. #
City	State/Prov.	Zip/Postal Code

Signature (if under 18, a parent or guardian must sign)

Mail to the **Reader Service:**
IN U.S.A.: P.O. Box 1867, Buffalo, NY 14240-1867
IN CANADA: P.O. Box 609, Fort Erie, Ontario L2A 5X3

* Terms and prices subject to change without notice. Prices do not include applicable taxes. Sales tax applicable in N.Y. Canadian residents will be charged applicable taxes. Offer not valid in Quebec. This offer is limited to one order per household. Not valid for current subscribers to Harlequin Heartwarming larger-print books. All orders subject to credit approval. Credit or debit balances in a customer's account(s) may be offset by any other outstanding balance owed by or to the customer. Please allow 4 to 6 weeks for delivery. Offer available while quantities last.

Your Privacy—The Reader Service is committed to protecting your privacy. Our Privacy Policy is available online at www.ReaderService.com or upon request from the Reader Service.

We make a portion of our mailing list available to reputable third parties that offer products we believe may interest you. If you prefer that we not exchange your name with third parties, or if you wish to clarify or modify your communication preferences, please visit us at www.ReaderService.com/consumerschoice or write to us at Reader Service Preference Service, P.O. Box 9062, Buffalo, NY 14240-9062. Include your complete name and address.

HWI5